THE LAST DAY

OF

HARRY CLARKE

A THREE-ACT PLAY

ANTHONY COSTIGAN

LUCY COSTIGAN

THERESA CULLEN

ENLIGHTEN PUBLISHING

DEDICATION

To Mam and Dad,
For a lifetime of support
And inspiration.

The Last Day of Harry Clarke
A Three-Act Play

Published 2019
By Enlighten Publishing,
14 Thomas Street,
Wexford,
Ireland

www.enlightenpublishing.com
www.harryclarke.net

Email: info@enlightenpublishing.com

ISBN: 978-0-9930188-1-7

ACKNOWLEDGEMENTS

In special memory of our dear friend, colleague and cousin, Raymond J. McGovern (1945-2019), for his significant role with the Harry Clarke team.

Thanks to Tony Walsh for editing the play and for constructive feedback. Thanks to Sharon and Martin Comerford for reading the first drafts and for sharing their helpful comments about text and cover.

Thank you to our families: to Sean for his supportive role; to Michael, Damien, Paul, Hilda, Calum, Isabelle, Brandon, Gemma and Tiny; to Kathleen, Sharon, Lisa, Antoinette, Martin and Aidan; to Jaden, Aidan Junior, Kenzie and Dylan; to Rocky—the great listener; in memory of Wilson—our loyal companion, and to Duke, our new friend; to Val, Yvonne, Alex, Christopher and Fiona; to Tony for all his support and companionship; to Lyiah for her understanding and thoughtful nature; to Lynsey and Sophie for being there when burning the midnight oil.

To a true teacher, Tom O'Connor, who inspired learning and curiosity.

CONTENTS

COVER PHOTOS

Front Cover: Train Station Arosa, Switzerland, Wlh. Halder, 1937; Drawing of H and C letters, original design by Theresa Cullen.

Back Cover: Sketch of Harry's Room in Davos by Anthony Costigan.

Cover Design: Michael Cullen (Irishimages.org)

PROLOGUE

Playwrights' Note

This is a stand-alone work that the general reader may enjoy as a fictionalised historical drama, based on the final day of Harry Clarke. Although it is a work of fiction, it is based on historically accurate facts of the period and all aspects of the setting and characters have been thoroughly researched. It is envisaged that it will be of particular interest to Harry Clarke aficionados.

With regard to Harry's state of mind during his last days in Davos, we took the view that the combination of the drugs he was taking to combat his illness, his frailty and his severe despondency with being so far from home may have created hallucinations so that at times he was not aware what was real and what was imaginary.

Although Lennox Robinson was not present in Davos with Harry Clarke on his final day, he was such a central part of Clarke's life and work that we felt it would have been a travesty to leave him out of any serious exploration of Harry Clarke. In the same vein, we felt that Harry's thoughts during those last days in Davos must have been brightened by memories of his great friend Lennox as the depth of their special friendship comes across clearly in their correspondence. Lennox had travelled to Davos with Harry during that arduous journey in October 1930 and it was he who had presented Harry with the special gift of a blue gramophone that is featured in the drama, to help him while away the hours. Thus, we hope our readers will forgive us this artistic licence.

Staging and Film Adaptation

This work is written as a three-act play for stage. Directors who are interested in staging the play for theatre or in adapting the work for film should contact the playwrights at: info@enlightenpublishing.com.

Characters

HARRY: Based on Harry Clarke, Irish stained-glass artist (1889 to 1931). Tall, with dark hair that has a tendency to fall over his brow. He is very thin, gaunt and ashen-faced. He is aged 41 years during the period when the play is set.

LENNOX: Based on Lennox Robinson (1886 to 1958), Irish playwright, producer and director, involved with the Abbey Theatre. He is tall and thin, with dark sandy hair and he wears round glasses. He speaks with a lilting Cork accent. He is 45 years old.

NURSE: Anna is Harry's nurse in the sanatorium. She is a pretty blond Swiss girl in her mid-20s. Her hair is arranged in a bun beneath her small, white nurse's cap. She wears a mid-length, high-necked, dark blue dress and a white apron. A watch is pinned to the bib of the apron.

JOSHUA: Based on Joshua Clarke (1858 to 1921), Harry's father. He is aged in his early 60s. He is originally from Leeds, in Yorkshire and still speaks with a strong Yorkshire accent, occasionally lapsing into the Yorkshire dialect. He is slightly bald and has a moustache. He is of average height and stocky build. He wears a dark suit, a waist coat with a watch chain and a hat.

PROFESSOR GAUCHE: The Professor is the Medical Director of the sanatorium. He is German and aged in his mid-50s. He has short grey hair and a well-shaped beard. He wears a white shirt and a dark three-piece suit with a pocket watch. His shoes are black patent. He is of average height and build, and is of military bearing. He wears a monocle in one eye and has a stethoscope around his neck.

DUNCAN: Based on Harry's friend, Alan Duncan (1895 to 1943). An Irishman, aged 36. He is tall and stands very erect, having been a captain in the British army during the First World War.

JOXER: Joxer Daly is the comic character from the play, *Juno and the Paycock* by Sean O'Casey. Depicted by Harry Clarke in the second section of the fourth panel, in *The Geneva* (1930).

DANCER: Beautiful blond female, naked, except for a diaphanous sheet that is draped around her. Based on a character from *Mr. Gilhooley* by Liam O'Flaherty. Depicted by Harry Clarke in the first scene of the sixth panel in *The Geneva Window* (1930).

THE WIDOW: Beautiful dark-haired woman, wearing a crimson dress and a long black cloak, decorated with white trimming. Her long dark hair is held in place with a crimson headdress. Depicted by Harry Clarke in the first section of the eighth panel in *The Geneva Window (1930)*.

MADELINE: Beautiful lady with long blond hair, wearing a white flowing nightgown and negligee. Depicted by Harry Clarke in *'The Eve of Saint Agnes'* (1924).

MOTHER: Harry Clarke's mother, Brigid Clarke (1860 to 1903), is in her early 40s, is of medium build, with grey hair arranged in a bun. She is dressed in a long blue robe.

STATIONMASTER: Middle-aged man with Swiss-German accent, of average build, wearing a blue uniform.

MEPHISTOPHELES: Devil in 'Faust' by Wolfgang Von Goethe, illustrated by Harry Clarke in 1925.

The Setting

Act One and Act Two are set in the St Victoria Sanatorium where tuberculosis patients are treated, in Davos, Switzerland. It is Monday, January 5th 1931, the last day of Harry Clarke's life. Act One, Scene One takes place in mid-morning while Scene Two takes place in the late morning. Scene Three is set in the late-afternoon. Act Two occurs in the evening.

Act Three, Scene One, is set in the stationmaster's office at the railway station in Arosa, Switzerland in the late evening. Act Three, Scene Two is set in a sanatorium in Arosa, Switzerland, in the early hours of Tuesday, January 6th 1931.

Act One and Act Two

The setting for the first two acts is Harry Clarke's room at the St Victoria Sanatorium. A set of double doors is located centre at the back of the stage. The view from the glass doors when opened shows a balcony and on the left, part of a divan which Harry is required to lie on as part of his treatment. In the distance are snow-capped mountains. In the evening scenes the lights of the town of Davos are visible in the skyline.

To the right of the double-doors is a white chest of drawers. On top of this is positioned a blue gramophone and a record rack, with a selection of 78 RPM (Revolutions Per Minute) vinyl records. There is also a silver framed photo of Harry's children. A large window with blinds is positioned to the right of the double-doors.

To the left of the double-doors there is a white bookcase. A glass vase filled with bluebells stands on top of the bookcase. A silver coloured carriage clock is also on the bookcase. Positioned over the bookcase is a mirror with a silver frame. There is also a large window with blinds to the left of the double-doors. A coat rack and a heater are located in front of the window.

A wardrobe is positioned near the corner of the left adjoining wall, beside the coat rack. A small waste bin is positioned beside the coat rack. The left adjoining wall features two doors. The first door, beside the wardrobe, leads to a bathroom. The second door is the main exit.

In the centre of the room, in front of the double doors, is a polished round table, an arm chair to the left and a smaller chair to the right. There is a fancy ink bottle half full of ink on the table with a fountain pen lying beside it. There are also several sheets of writing paper, envelopes, some blotting paper and a blue strand of ribbon. There are some rolled up balls of paper on the side of the table, some of which have rolled onto the floor near the waste paper basket, beside the coat rack.

A bed is positioned parallel to the right window with the head resting at the adjoining right wall. Two small lockers are located beside the bed. The locker to the left of the bed contains a carafe full of water, a glass, some handkerchieves, an ashtray, a medicine bottle, a spoon and a pill box. The locker to the right contains a bedside lamp. A small chair is located beside the right window, facing the bed. The bed has white sheets and pillows, and a light blue blanket on top. A painting of a snow scene is hanging on the wall to the right of the window.

An electric light with a glass shade hangs down over the table. The floor is covered with lino.

Act Three, Scene One
Act Three, Scene One is set in the Stationmaster's office in the railway station at Arosa, Switzerland. It is late evening. The office is furnished with a pot-bellied stove, left of centre. A pot of coffee sits on the stove. There are three chairs positioned close to the wall at the back of the

room, to the right of the stove. There is a door to the left that leads onto the platform. Above the chairs, there is a painting of a train on the wall, an old wooden clock and a sign printed with the word 'Arosa'. There are shelves at either side of the painting. Several tins and some mugs are on the shelves. There is a long table to the front of the room, containing a lamp and stationery. The sound of the old clock ticking can be heard.

Act Three, Scene Two

Act Three, Scene Two is set in a sanatorium in Arosa, Switzerland, in the early hours of January 6th 1931. The room is sparsely decorated. There is one large window in the centre. HARRY's bed is positioned to the left of the room, with the back of the bed at the left wall. There is a small locker beside the bed, to HARRY's left, that contains a carafe of water and a glass. Two armchairs are positioned to the right of the room. There is also a small table positioned in front of the chairs in the centre of the room. There is a small press at the right corner of the room with a pot of coffee on top. A number of cases, coats and bags are lying by the wall, to the right of the room. The room is lit by a small lamp on the table, leaving the further reaches of the room in partial darkness.

THE LAST DAY OF HARRY CLARKE

ACT ONE

Scene One

Lights up on HARRY's *room in the sanatorium. There is a song playing on the gramophone, 'Bye Bye Blackbird' (1926), beginning from 'Pack up all my cares and woes'. The song continues to play in the background until it ends. It is mid-morning.* HARRY *is coughing and spluttering. The double doors are open.* HARRY *has just come in from the balcony carrying a sketchbook under his arm and a blanket. He places the blanket across the foot of the bed. He goes over to the bedside locker positioned to the left of the bed and fills out a glass of water from the carafe. He takes a drink of water and replaces the glass on the locker. He gets a fit of coughing. His sketchbook falls to the floor. In a moment of frustration he picks up his sketchbook, tears out a sheet, rolls it up and flings it towards the waste bin. He misses. He throws the sketchbook onto the table.*

HARRY. God damn it, what's the use?

> HARRY *pulls off his gloves, cap, scarf and coat. He stuffs the gloves, cap and scarf into the pockets of his coat and then hangs up the coat on the rack. He is*

wearing a royal blue silk robe over cotton pyjamas and dark blue slippers. He puts his hand to his chest as he tries to catch his breath.

He takes a few deep breaths, trying to steady himself. He walks over to the chest of drawers and stares wistfully at the photo of his children. He lifts up the photo. He turns around, still holding the photo and touches it delicately.

(Lovingly) Oh my little ones! How I miss you so much.

After a few moments **HARRY** *replaces the photo. He absentmindedly opens the second drawer and takes out a packet of cigarettes and a lighter. He lights a cigarette. He inhales and then gets a fit of coughing. He goes over to the open doors in obvious frustration, then throws the cigarette out over the balcony.*

Blast it! I can't even enjoy a smoke anymore!

HARRY *closes the double doors. He throws the cigarettes and the lighter back into the drawer. The music has ended so he puts the needle of the gramophone back into its holder. Then he makes his way over to the table and sits in the small chair. He takes up a writing pad and begins to write.*

After a few moments there is a sharp knock on the door. HARRY *stops writing and looks up towards the door.*

(*Looking up*) Who is it?

NURSE. It is I, Monsieur, Nurse Anna.

HARRY. Oh! Come in Anna!

NURSE *enters.*

NURSE. Ah, Monsieur Clarke, how are you feeling this morning?

HARRY. (*Smiling weakly, his left hand rubbing his forehead*) Ah! I'm not great nurse.

HARRY *watches* NURSE *as she sniffs the air and shakes her head.*

NURSE. (*Seriously*) Mm, I'm sure de smoking does not help, Monsieur.

HARRY. Would you believe Anna, I couldn't smoke even if I tried, with this damned coughing. (*Mischievously grinning*) And I have tried, believe me! (*Pushing back his chair and standing up, beginning to pace up and down*).

NURSE. You must be careful that de Professor does not detect any smoke.

HARRY. (*Shaking his head, determinedly*) Well, right now Anna I'm not too worried about the Professor, I can tell you! If only Duncan would get here soon I'd be on my way out of here.

NURSE. (*A little irritated*) You keep saying you are leaving, Monsieur Clarke. (*She walks over to the doors and opens them*). You know you will need to talk to de Professor before making any arrangements.

HARRY. (*Stopping to look at* NURSE *as she settles the bed*) I'll tell the Professor when everything is in place, don't you worry Anna.

HARRY *coughs again, then goes back to sit down at the table.*

(*Thinking aloud, fiddling with the pen, his left hand on his forehead*) That reminds me, there are a few friends from the Irish Circle I'd like to see before I go. I must say they're a grand lot. Can't say I haven't enjoyed the chats with OJ, Mansergh and the boys. (*Looking directly at* NURSE) But I'm so restless now Anna, I just need to get home (*coughing, putting a handkerchief to his mouth*).

NURSE. (*Settling the pillows*) You are in a very strange humour today, Monsieur Clarke. (*Turning back to look at* HARRY) Maybe you need to rest more.

HARRY. (*Shaking his head slowly*) It's not rest I need Anna. I'm just not getting any better–you more than anyone should know that. (*Pause*) I won't be sorry to see the back of this place, I can tell you. It's all so colourless here–the mountains, the fields, the sky–even the walls, all silver, grey and white. Sporty types may find this spectacular but for me it's become monotonous. This pale insipid palette is draining my very life's blood!

NURSE. (*Going back over to close the doors*) But you know the air is so clear here.

HARRY. I know, I know all that. (*Opening his arms wide as though praying*) Davos is where the sadly afflicted gather in search of a cure, an elixir to heal all their ills. (*Becoming deadly serious*) But we know Anna that very few are ever healed. I know you can't admit it, but I'm not a daw. I know what goes on here some nights, when people suddenly disappear. Like Heir Muller last week–one day he was in his room, looking as white as a ghost and coughing up his guts, then the next day he was gone. Were we supposed to believe he had suddenly been cured and had returned home to Deutschland? I think not, Anna.

NURSE. (*Flustered*) I...I don't know, Monsieur Clarke. Some people are cured. The air helps people to breathe better.

HARRY. (*Sarcastically*) I've been lying out on that divan in sub-zero temperatures, wrapped up like a mummy for the past three months! I can't sketch with those damn gloves on, not that there's much to sketch anyway. (*Coughing and trying to catch his breath*) All I know is that I'm getting worse.

NURSE *tops up the glass of water from the carafe on the locker. She walks over to* HARRY, *carrying the glass.*

HARRY. I need to be home Anna…and I need my work.

HARRY *takes a sip of water and then puts the glass down on the table.*

My sister Dolly wrote again, asking for the preliminary drawings for 'The Last Judgement'. 'Tis right up my alley, you know Anna, *(smirking)* dredging up devils and demons.

NURSE. But who would want such a window? (*She takes up the glass from the table and carries it back over to the locker).*

HARRY. You'd be surprised what people want, especially the religious. They need their hellish torments you know to frighten their flock into submission.

NURSE. (*Walking over to the table*) I don't like to think about such things.

HARRY. But Anna, to really get people's attention, the window needs to balance the light of goodness with the blackest pits of sin.

NURSE. You look tired. Maybe you need to get back into bed.

HARRY. No. I need to write to my children. (*Mopping his brow with a handkerchief*) I don't think I can sleep until I write to them.

NURSE. (*Annoyed*) I cannot get any good of you today, Monsieur.

HARRY. Ah, all right then Anna. (*Smiling*) Maybe a little nap, just for you!

NURSE. (*Brightening up*) Yes, Monsieur Harry, you can finish your letter later. (*Helping to take off* HARRY's *dressing gown*) What a beautiful dressing gown Monsieur. A gift perhaps?

HARRY. Yes indeed Anna. My sisters sent it over for Christmas.

NURSE. (*Hanging the dressing gown on the hook to the right of the bed*) Such a lovely colour!

HARRY. Ah yes, deep blue, my favourite.

HARRY *takes off his slippers and leaves them beside the bed.* NURSE *then helps* HARRY *to get into bed. He coughs again and holds a handkerchief over his mouth.*

NURSE *pours him a glass of water from the carafe.*
HARRY *takes a sip.*

NURSE. Are your family well, Monsieur?

HARRY. They are, thanks Anna. I got a letter from Margaret yesterday. She met our good friend Lennox before Christmas and they both think I should stay here. They believe it's for the best. I don't share that belief any more. (HARRY *smiles wistfully and gestures towards the photo on the chest of drawers*). She said the children really miss me, those dear little sweet ones. I think of them so often. (*Looking upwards, reminiscing*) Last night I dreamt we were out in the garden back home in Dublin and they were clambering all over me, having a rip roaring time. I was sure I felt their tiny arms locked around my neck, and their little hands placed securely in mine.

NURSE. (*Going over to the chest of drawers to look at the photo*) They are beautiful children.

HARRY. Yes they are.

HARRY coughs again. NURSE *takes a thermometer out of her apron pocket. She proceeds to take* HARRY's *temperature. After a few seconds she removes the thermometer and takes a reading. She records this on the chart by the bed.*

NURSE. I see you haven't filled in your temperature chart Monsieur Harry. Professor Gauche will be doing the rounds later and you know how he likes everything to be exact.

HARRY. Oh! The illustrious Herr Eric Van Botch!

NURSE. (*Trying to stifle a laugh*) Monsieur Harry, at times you are just too much.

HARRY. Well 'tis in the Professor's interest to keep me hale and hearty since I'm worth more to him alive than dead!

NURSE *smiles, shakes her head and turns to leave.*

HARRY. (*Beseechingly*) Anna, don't go yet. Stay and talk for a while?

NURSE. Well, you need to get plenty of rest and I have so much work to do...But I will stay just a little while more.

NURSE *sits down on the chair beside the bed.*

HARRY. (*Resting back on his pillow*) Thank you, Anna. You have always been so good to me.

NURSE *smiles at him. She looks at the watch that is pinned to her apron, picks up* HARRY's *left hand and* proceeds *to take his pulse.*

HARRY. (*Longingly*) I wish you'd known me when I was in my prime, Anna. Imagine if we'd have met back then, we could have been out on the town, wining and dining in all the best clubs in London, having the time of our lives in the grandest theatres. Attending concerts and ballets at the Alhambra, you dressed like a countess in black satin and pearls, then later dancing cheek to cheek in Murray's.

HARRY's *breathing becomes laboured again.*

NURSE *lets go of* HARRY's *hand. She takes up the glass of water and gives it to* HARRY. *He takes a few sips then puts it back down on the locker.*

NURSE. (*Shaking her head*) My, you are de dreamer, Monsieur Harry.

HARRY. But I am serious, Anna. You could have been my muse. No other woman could possess such a saint's soul and an angel's face.

HARRY *reaches to touch her face.* NURSE *draws away, smiling.*

Your beauty, dear Anna, is both inward and outward. You would have graced the central light of my finest window, with your long flowing hair, your hazel eyes and your small ruby lips.

NURSE. (*Blushing shyly*) Monsieur Harry, you are a poet like all Irish men; making love to every woman you meet. Very charming, yes, but very dangerous too for a simple Swiss girl. (*Smoothing down her apron*) Maybe I will wear my face mask in future as you seem to be spending so much of the time praising me. I really should be wearing it but often I forget.

NURSE *pulls a mask out of her pocket and holds it up to her mouth, teasingly, then she smiles and tucks it back into her pocket.*

HARRY. (*Smiling*) What a pity that would be, Anna!

NURSE *takes up a spoon and a bottle of medicine from the bedside locker.* HARRY *scrunches up his face.*

HARRY. (*In mock protest*) Ah! Not that vile concoction!

NURSE *pours the medicine onto the spoon and then holds the spoon up to his mouth.* HARRY *swallows.*

HARRY. Yuck!

NURSE. Doctor's orders! Now, try to get some rest. You can dream of all those angels you keep telling me about.

HARRY. (*Teasingly*) Do you mind if I include you in my dreams?

NURSE. (*Replacing the medicine and spoon on the locker*) You are always so funny, Monsieur!

HARRY. Seriously Anna, I would dearly love to show you my windows: virgins and queens; knights and princesses. And the Lady Madeline from *The Eve of Saint Agnes.*

NURSE. You have promised to show them to me many times. Maybe one day I will see them.

HARRY. I hope so, Anna, I hope so.

NURSE. All right, Monsieur Harry. I'll look in on you again later, just to check how you are feeling and to see if you need any further medication for the night. I am just going to pull the blinds now. It will be easier for you to sleep.

HARRY. You have been so kind to me Anna and you have perked me up as only you can.

NURSE *pulls the blinds down half way on both windows. The room darkens.*

NURSE. (*Smiling*) Don't you know it is all part of an angel's work! Sweet dreams, Monsieur Harry. NURSE *exits through the main door.*

HARRY *drifts off to sleep.*

Scene Two

HARRY's Room, with JOSHUA, HARRY's *father, walking in from the darkened left-hand corner. It is late morning. JOSHUA takes off his hat and then looks around the room. HARRY is asleep in bed, lying on his left side, facing towards the audience, his head resting on his left hand. JOSHUA walks over to the bed and places his hat on the floor beside the chair.*

JOSHUA. 'arry, lad! (*Shaking* HARRY *gently)* I made it. I've come ta visit. I told you I'd not let ye down.

HARRY. Wha..What?...(*rubbing his eyes).*

JOSHUA. (*Tipping him on the shoulder*) It's me 'arry, your Pop!

HARRY. Pop? (*Turning slowly towards* JOSHUA). It can't be! (*Slowly opening his eyes and squinting as he tries to focus in the darkened room).* But it is you! (*Looking dazed but delighted).*

JOSHUA. I told ye I'd come!

HARRY. Pop, I...I can't believe it! (*Smiling joyfully and half-sitting up in bed)* Ah! It's so good to hear your voice again...that Yorkshire lilt never sounded so good. (*Laughing through his tears while reaching to embrace his father)* I've missed you so, Pop.

31

JOSHUA. (*Sitting down on the bedside chair and putting his hand on* HARRY's *shoulder*) I'm chuffed to see ye too lad. Now, just lie back for a while and try to rest.

HARRY. I've never needed you more Pop.

HARRY *starts coughing. He pulls out a handkerchief and holds it up to his mouth, still coughing.* JOSHUA *places a hand on* HARRY's *shoulder.* HARRY *reaches for the glass of water and takes a sip. After a few moments* HARRY's *coughing subsides.*

HARRY. I'm not too good Pop. I've been here for months now and I'm not getting any better. I'm worried Pop and I'm fearful…*(Putting his hands over his face)*…and the business…Oh! God, I don't know what I'm going to do? Somehow I have to get home and sort things out…My mind is in turmoil, Pop. I think I'm taking leave of my senses, what, with the strange concoctions they're giving me and then the constant worry. (*Looking up anxiously at his father*) I just don't think I can take much more.

JOSHUA. (*Caringly*) I know 'arry. You've been right poorly. I can see thee needs tendin' to, lad, and I'm here for ye now, so try not to worry so much about things. All will be well soon.

HARRY. (*Brightening up a little*) It's so good to talk to you again, Pop.

HARRY *coughs into his handkerchief.*

JOSHUA (*Pulling his coat tighter around him and blowing on his hands*) Hey, it's a might frozen in here 'arry.

HARRY. (*Pulling the blankets up higher*) Too true, Pop. It takes some getting used to, I can tell you. The heating doesn't come on until evening, unless there's a heavy snow...They like us to spend as much time as possible outside, you know.

JOSHUA. (*Putting his hands under his arms*) How do you stick it, lad?

HARRY. (*Beckoning towards the locker*) Take a look in the locker, Pop. (*Sitting up in bed, looking a little more cheerful*) You'll find a little something to warm us up.

JOSHUA (*Reaching over to the locker and stooping down,* JOSHUA *reaches inside the locker and pulls out a bottle of whiskey and two glasses*) Now, that's what I call a medicine cabinet, lad.

JOSHUA *gives a glass to* HARRY.

HARRY. (*Frowning, while looking at the glass*) Well, maybe just a small one then, Pop.

33

JOSHUA *chuckles, then proceeds to pour out the whiskey. He places the bottle on top of the locker.*

JOSHUA. That's right, 'arry. Your ol' man knows best. Sure that little 'un won't do ye any 'arm. It'll warm y'up. *(Toasting)* To kit and kin!

HARRY: Kit and Kin!

HARRY *and* JOSHUA *clink their glasses and sip the whiskey.*

HARRY. (*Grinning mischievously*) You know Pop, I have a few bottles stashed in various locations. Lennox always manages to bring me some goodies when he visits.

JOSHUA. (*Chuckling*) Aye, lad. You two 'ave always been inseparable. 'e 'as always been a true friend to you and Margaret.

HARRY. (*Sincerely*) I just don't know what we'd have done without him, Pop. He's been such a help to us in our time of need. And Duncan has also been tremendous. He's coming here to accompany me back home, you know, Pop.

JOSHUA. Aye, lad, I know. It'll be a treacherous journey but don't fret; you'll eventually arrive safely home.

HARRY. Thanks Pop.

JOSHUA. Ah, I'm warmin' up now lad, but maybe I'll just have another little 'un for the road. (*Pouring the whiskey into his glass, beckoning to* HARRY) Care to join me, 'arry?

HARRY. No thanks, Pop, I'm afraid there's no over-indulgence here! But 'tis grand to have a chance to talk to you again.

JOSHUA. 'Tis grand, son. (*Standing up and stretching, then picking up the whiskey glass from the locker*) Have you been sketchin' a lot since you got 'ere, 'arry? (*Strolling across the room*) Knowin' you, you're burstin' with ideas as ever, lad.

HARRY *throws off the covers and gets out of bed. He puts on his slippers then takes his dressing-gown from the hook beside the bed. He begins to cough.*

JOSHUA. Nay, lad, there's no need for ye to get up.

HARRY. (*Coughing, walking over to the chest of drawers*) That's all right, Pop. I just want to show you some of my drawings. I've been doin' little else here except sketching. (*Pulling out three sketchbooks from the chest of drawers*) Take a look, Pop.

HARRY *puts the sketchbooks on the table.* JOSHUA *comes over to the table, sits down, puts his whiskey glass on the table and begins looking through the sketches.*

HARRY *goes back over to the bedside locker, still coughing, takes up the medicine bottle and drinks from it.* HARRY *keeps his eyes glued to* JOSHUA *who is looking through the sketches, shaking his head and smiling to himself.*

JOSHUA. (*Turning to look over at* HARRY) Are you all right there, son?

HARRY. I'm all right now, Pop.

> HARRY's *coughing subsides. He walks across to the table and stands behind* JOSHUA, *his hand resting on the back of his chair.*
>
> That's the Newport design for the record-keepers in 'The Last Judgement'.

JOSHUA. Aye, lad, truly marvellous work as ever.

JOSHUA *takes a sip of whiskey.* HARRY *walks slowly to the front of the room, becoming lost in thought. He puts his hands in his pockets.*

HARRY. You know Pop, I often think about the old days and all the work you did to keep the business goin'. I was so focused on my own work back then that I often took you for granted, (*glancing over at* JOSHUA *who is still absorbed in the sketchbooks*) thinking you'd always be there. (*Pausing for a moment, then looking outwards*) You were a great manager, Pop and a gifted

36

craftsman in your own right. I could never get all the orders that you got. Why, you even won the great Mansion House commission. Remember Pop?

JOSHUA. (*Looking up at* HARRY) Aye, I did well enough, though Mr. Yeats mightn't agree.

HARRY. (*Turning towards* JOSHUA) Ah, forget what W.B said. He should have stuck to his rhyming couplets and let us get on with our art! (*Looking upwards*) Oh! What great days they were, Pop. Sure, you had taken over most of the church decorating work in the city. Not bad for a simple Yorkshire lad, (*Turning again towards* JOSHUA) eh, Pop? (*Laughing*).

JOSHUA *looks up at* HARRY *and picks up his glass.*

JOSHUA *stands up and walks over to* HARRY, *positioning himself slightly left of centre.*

JOSHUA. It was grand, lad. Mr. Yeats may 'ave believed I was as daft as a brush but I showed 'im lad.

HARRY. (*Looking upwards in thought*) What a team we were, eh, Pop? You, me, Dolly, Lally and Walter; all throwin' in our lot. We were untouchable!

JOSHUA. (*Grinning with satisfaction*) Aye, indeed lad, indeed.

There is silence for a few moments as they both become

37

lost in thought.

HARRY. (*Looking directly at* JOSHUA, *beaming*) Hey, Pop, remember our days in Paris?

JOSHUA. (*Placing a hand on* HARRY's *shoulder*) Oh aye! Sure that was the best trip I ever took. You had won that scholarship. Oh, I was so proud of ye, son.

HARRY. Yes, Pop, I can still see the medieval windows of Notre Dame in the early morning light? (*Pause*) Those magnificent deep, rich colours.

As HARRY *is speaking, the room becomes darkened and the faint sound of Gregorian chant can be head.*

The double doors suddenly become transformed into exquisite stained-glass windows. JOSHUA, *positioned left of centre, takes a few steps further left, turning sideways to stare at the windows.* HARRY, *positioned right of centre, takes a few steps right, turning sideways and becoming transfixed by the windows. The figure of Christ in ruby robes is displayed in the first light, while the Virgin Mary dressed in a dark blue cloak and surrounded by angels is depicted in the second light.*

JOSHUA. (*Speaking in a hushed tone, as though in church*) Aye lad, they were masters all right, those mediaeval craftsmen.

HARRY. Gosh, we must have sat there for hours, Pop? Staring, then scribbling notes, trying to get up close to the glass, to take in every last detail. How to create those colours, that was the great mystery to unravel?

The images begin to fade. JOSHUA *and* HARRY *turn back to face each other.*

JOSHUA. (*Delighted*) Ah, but you did crack it, lad. Ha! Marvellous shades you got of every colour under the sun.

HARRY. (*Dreamily, looking upwards*) You remember, Pop, all the hours I spent in the Studio, trying to perfect aciding and plating? And the colours did finally emerge - purples and gold, deep shades of orange, emerald, ruby and every shade of blue.

JOSHUA. Aye, lad, truly amazing they were.

HARRY. (*Looking directly at* JOSHUA) I could never have achieved what I did without you, Pop. You supported me in every possible way.

JOSHUA. (*Looking at* HARRY) I did me best for ye all, but I always knew you were a mite special, ever since you were a lad.

HARRY. (*Teasing*) And remember how we'd compete for commissions, Pop?

JOSHUA. *(Shaking his head and smiling to himself)* Aye, but you nearly always won, son. Still kept ye sharp, though; kept ye on your toes.

HARRY: Oh! How I wish we could go back to those days again, Pop.

HARRY *places an arm around* JOSHUA's *shoulder.*
HARRY and JOSHUA *walk slowly back to the bed.*
HARRY *takes off his dressing gown and places it on the hook. He places his slippers under the bed on the right hand side.* JOSHUA *sits back on the chair, putting the whiskey glass back on the locker.* HARRY *gets back into bed. The room begins to gradually darken.*

HARRY. *(Smiling)* So Pop, are you still smoking that old pipe? Oh! How I miss the smell of that tobacco.

JOSHUA. Aye lad, I am indeed. *(Reaching inside his pocket and taking out his pipe)* I'm not about to light it 'ere though 'arry. *(Chuckling)* I don't think the nurse will be very impressed some 'ow.

JOSHUA *absentmindedly taps the bowl into the ashtray...tap, tap, tap. Simultaneously there are three taps at the door.*

HARRY *turns over onto his left side. Suddenly he is slumbering deeply, his head resting on his left hand. The room darkens while light falls on* HARRY's *face.*

Then there are a further three taps at the door. A voice accompanies the taps.

LENNOX. Harry, old man, 'tis I, Lennox!

HARRY. (*Groggily, rubbing his eyes*) Wha...what? (*Waking up*) Pop! (*Speaking louder now, dramatically lifting his head off the pillow*) Pop!

HARRY *turns swiftly around in bed, then stares at the empty chair, looking agitated.* HARRY *slowly slumps down on the pillow, looking dejected. He closes his eyes and puts his hands over his face.*

(*Sadly*) My God!

HARRY *groans, puts his hands down, then slowly raises his head, shaking it in disbelief as he looks from the empty chair to the locker that is now without the glasses and the whiskey bottle. A rueful expression is on his face.*

There is further tapping and HARRY *looks towards the door.*

(*Groggy and confused, turning on the light*) Yes, eh...who is it?

LENNOX. 'Tis I, Clarke, Lennox...Are you all right, old man? (*Impatiently*) Are you going to let me in?

HARRY. (*Struggling to grasp the situation*) What? (*Excitedly*) My dear friend, I can't believe it. (*Getting out of bed*) I...I'll be right there.

HARRY *bends down at the right side of the bed to put on his slippers. Then he picks up his dressing gown from the hook beside his bed, struggles into it as he stumbles across the room towards the door.* HARRY *opens the door.* LENNOX *steps into the room with a suitcase. He puts down the suitcase and embraces* HARRY.

LENNOX. (*Warmly*) My old friend, how are you keeping?

HARRY. (*Looking a bit sheepish*) I'm frightfully sorry, Lennox. I was in such a deep sleep. (*Leading* LENNOX *across the room*) Please forgive me!

LENNOX. Ah think nothing of it, old boy!

HARRY *shakes his head as he looks over at the empty chair by the bed.*

HARRY. I only hope I'm not still dreaming.

LENNOX. (*Chuckling*) Whatever are you talking about Clarke? Just what kind of medicine are they giving you? (*Smiling*) I might try some of it myself.

LENNOX *puts his arm around* HARRY's *shoulder and gives it a squeeze.*

It's great to see you again, old boy!

HARRY. *(Staring at* LENNOX*)* Sorry Lennox, you must be frozen. Hang up your coat there while I get you a drop of the owld crater to warm you up.

LENNOX *picks up his case and walks towards the coat rack.* LENNOX *puts down his case beside it. He takes off his hat and heavy coat and puts his scarf and gloves in his pocket. He hangs them on the coat rack.*

Simultaneously, HARRY *walks over to the locker. Then* LENNOX *walks over to the radiator and warms his hands while* HARRY *opens the locker, stooping to take out the unopened whiskey bottle.*

LENNOX *(Turning around, warming his back on the radiator)* Gosh Harry, I forgot how cold it is here.

HARRY *scratches his head as he stares at the whiskey bottle in his hand and then looks at the chair.*

LENNOX. Hey, old man, are you just going to look at that bottle all night or are you going to open it?

HARRY. Oh! Eh…why, yes… yes of course. *(Looking a little disorientated)* I'll just get the glasses.

HARRY *takes out two glasses and he beckons to* LENNOX *to sit in the arm chair by the table.* LENNOX *sits down.* HARRY *then brings the whiskey bottle and the glasses over to the table and pours two drinks, handing one to* LENNOX.

LENNOX. Bottoms up!

HARRY *and* LENNOX *both take a drink.* HARRY *sits down in the opposite chair.*

LENNOX. My word, but that's fine whiskey, if I may say so.

HARRY. Well, you may say so since it was you who sent it over!

LENNOX. Well, to your good health, Harry.

HARRY. You always had a queer sense of humour.

HARRY *and* LENNOX *clink their glasses and take a few sips.*

(*Relaxing*) So Lennox, you never mentioned you were coming here. It's more than I could have hoped for.

LENNOX. (*Rubbing his hands together, still trying to get warm*) Well, old boy, I've just come from Paris. I took a detour through the Alps, just to see your bemused expression when I turned up on your doorstep.

HARRY *starts coughing.*

LENNOX. Are you all right, old man?

LENNOX *stands up but* HARRY *waves him away.*

HARRY. I'm all right. Just give me a minute.

HARRY *gets up slowly and walks over to the locker. He coughs intermittently. He takes up a handkerchief and puts it in his pocket. He takes a drink from the medicine bottle, scrunching up his face as he swallows. Then he pours some water into a glass from the carafe.*

Simultaneously, LENNOX *strolls over to the chest of drawers. He flicks through the records, selects one and begins reading the back of the sleeve.*

HARRY *walks back towards the table, carrying the water glass.*

LENNOX. *(Looking over at* HARRY*)* Are you all right, old man?

HARRY. Oh, I'm all right now, it's just that confounded cough. (*Looking towards the gramophone*) Put something on, Lennox, to liven the place up a bit. You know, your gift of that gramophone is one of the reasons I'm still sane. More than anything, it helps to pass away the dull evenings.

LENNOX. (*Nodding)* I knew you'd enjoy listening to all your favourites.

LENNOX *puts the record on the turntable and turns the gramophone's handle. Then he places the needle on the first groove of the record. A pleasant orchestral piece reminiscent of band music circa 1929 plays in the background.* LENNOX *remains standing.*

HARRY *sits down at the table and takes another sip of water.*

HARRY. (*Warily*) So, er, did you meet up with Duncan in Paris?

LENNOX. No, I didn't get a chance to see him.

HARRY. (*Cupping his hands around the water glass*) Oh! He's coming here you know.

LENNOX. (*Surprised*) Oh! Is he?

HARRY. (*Hesitantly, casting his eyes downwards, playing with the glass*) Yes, I'm expecting him at any moment as a matter of fact. (*Looking up at LENNOX*) He's…eh…coming to take me home.

LENNOX *slowly turns towards HARRY, putting his hands on his hips, then standing completely still, staring at him, raising his voice in shock.*

LENNOX. What? Tell me you're not serious.

HARRY. (*Defensively*) Well, you know I've been thinking about this…since the first day I got here. (*Putting a handkerchief to his mouth to stifle a cough*) It was a mistake, Lennox, to ever come back here. Everyone means well but…I…I need to get home. I can't stand it here. I've made up my mind.

LENNOX *walks smartly over to the gramophone, takes up the arm from the record and replaces it in its holder.*

The music stops abruptly.

LENNOX. *(Annoyed)* You can't be thinking of leaving in your condition. You know how rough the journey is across those mountains in the height of winter. I've just travelled over that treacherous terrain. It's foolhardy for you to even think about it. (*Pacing up and down the room*) It's the first I've heard of it. I can't believe Duncan would be involved in hatching such a damnable plan, especially without talking it over with me. Damn, it must be the only time I didn't call to see him when I was in Paris.

HARRY. (*Downcast*) I'm sorry, Lennox. I knew how you'd feel. You're the best friend in the world and you always mean so well, but...you see, I have to go. (*Becoming more animated*) Can you begin to understand? No matter what happens I need to try to get back...to the children, to the family, to Margaret, to try to sort out some of the work that's piling up, and to find out once and for all what's happening with *The Geneva Window.*

LENNOX. (Facing HARRY, *leaning with both hands on the table,* exasperated) Do you think Margaret or your sisters or anyone would agree to you travelling across the Alps at this time of year in your state of health? I can only imagine what they'd say to me if I was party to such folly.

HARRY. (*Suddenly downcast*) I haven't told anyone yet Lennox but…I finally got the truth out of Old Botch and…there's been irreparable damage done…it's highly unlikely I'll be getting any better. So it's lunacy to stay here, what, with the cost of the place and the distance I am from the Studios. I'm of no use to anyone sitting here day after day. I've already written to tell them I'm leaving once Duncan arrives. Nothing will change that now.

LENNOX *sighs, straightens up and then walks over to* HARRY, *placing a hand on his shoulder. They both remain silent for a few moments. Then* LENNOX *takes up the whiskey bottle from the table and pours himself a drink. He beckons towards* HARRY's *glass but* HARRY *shakes his head.* LENNOX *sits back down in the chair.*

LENNOX. You were always the stubborn one, always had to get your own way. What am I going to do with you, Harry? I don't like this, I don't agree with any of it. I feel somewhat responsible if you leave here and go trudging through the snow.

HARRY. Like Porphyro?

LENNOX. (*Annoyed*) Very funny Harry but you know it's no laughing matter.

HARRY. (*Sincere*) You've always been there for me Lennox. The best friend any man could ever have. I know conditions are not ideal but...

LENNOX. (*Sarcastically*) Ideal? That's a laugh!

HARRY. I have to get home Lennox. It's my only chance...

LENNOX. Knowing you, it doesn't matter what I say. (*Pausing*) I'll help you in any way I can, but I'm worried what's in store, how you're going to stand up to such a journey in the middle of winter.

HARRY. I know how you feel, Lennox. I can see you're worried but we'll have Duncan to help and the three of us are dynamite when we're together. Why, we could...move mountains (*slight snigger, raising his shoulders*).

LENNOX. Yes and I'll be having a few choice words with our Captain Duncan when I see him.

HARRY It's all my doing Lennox. Don't be too hard on Duncan. Who else would I ask to help me but my two best friends?

LENNOX. (*Shaking his head and rubbing his forehead*) God, Harry. It's always so hard to stay angry with you for long.

HARRY. Let's see if the liquor can make you mellow.

HARRY *tops up* LENNOX*'s glass, then lowers his voice.*

Oh! I've seen you angry before. (*Smiling*) Remember that time in Tangier?

LENNOX. Tangier?

HARRY. (*Raising his eyebrows, smiling*) When a certain valise went missing?

LENNOX. (*Sipping the whiskey, then raising his voice in mock anger*) You mean when 'you' lost my valise! I was beside myself—all those notes for my new play, all vanished into thin air.

HARRY. (*Laughing*) But somehow we ended up rolling in the sand, laughing our heads off. But as I recall the liquor and cigars helped to revive your drooping spirit, eventually.

LENNOX. (*Taking a drink*) It'll take a lot of liquor before I can laugh this one off Harry. (*Sighing*) But I know you'll follow this through and somehow—as usual—you'll persuade me to play a part.

HARRY. Well, let's call a truce then. (*Taking up the whiskey glass and raising it*) To adventures, my friend!

LENNOX. (*Hesitantly raising his glass*) To cracked

schemes!

HARRY *and* LENNOX *both sip their whiskey. They sit in silence for a few moments.*

HARRY. So tell me, Lennox, isn't your play opening in the Abbey this week? When do you need to get back?

LENNOX. (*Distracted*) It opens tomorrow night and runs for two weeks.

HARRY. God, it's incredible you'd miss your opening night, Lennox, to come all the way out here just to visit me. (*Excited*) Sure, if we leave right away when Duncan arrives you'll get to see some of the performances and he could arrive at any time.

LENNOX. (*Sarcastically*) Well, I must admit it was touch and go whether I'd miss the early performances and now that I've heard the full story I'm not sure I made the right decision. (*Yawning*) Anyway, old man, I've just got here, I'm tired and hungry and I need to find somewhere to stay. When Duncan arrives we'll trash everything out. But now I need to get a hearty meal. Do you want to come down to the dining room?

HARRY. No, Lennox. I think I'll stay here. I've things to sort out.

LENNOX. (*Gently*) Maybe try to get some rest. Shall I bring you back something then?

HARRY. Oh! Yes, all right, something light perhaps. And maybe a glass of milk if it's not too much trouble. You'll be back then Lennox?

LENNOX. Of course! See you later, old man.

Lights down.

Scene Three

Lights up on HARRY's *Room in the sanatorium. It is late afternoon. The second door on the left is open. The sound of water running and intermittent coughing can be heard from the bathroom.* HARRY *comes out fixing his tie. He is wearing a white shirt and black trousers. He goes to the wardrobe, takes out a black suit jacket and puts it on. He then goes to the mirror and combs his unruly hair. He steps back and stretches out his arms in a mock religious gesture.*

HARRY. An improvement, to be sure! The dead arose and appeared to many.

HARRY *nods and smiles sarcastically. He goes back to the table and pours himself a small whiskey and returns to the mirror, raising his glass in a toast.*

I drink to your health when I'm with you. I drink to your health when I'm alone. I drink to your health so often I'm starting to worry about my own.

HARRY *laughs a little to himself at this. He takes a sip. He turns and slowly paces the room in a thoughtful mood. Then he goes to the table which contains a sketch pad, a pen, an ink bottle, some blotting paper and a blue strand of ribbon. He puts down his drink. He opens the sketch pad and removes a sketch. He picks up the sketch and holds it up to the light, scrutinising it for a few moments. Then he gives a nod of satisfaction before placing it back on the table. He takes up his fountain pen, then looks up thoughtfully for a moment. He leans over the table then writes something on the sketch, signing it with a flourish. He then puts some blotting paper over the writing. He picks the sketch up once again and blows on it. Then he carefully rolls it up on the table and ties it with the blue ribbon. He walks over to the double doors and opens them. He takes out a cigarette from a silver case and a lighter from his pocket, and he lights the cigarette. He takes a few puffs and then begins to cough.*

Damn it!

HARRY *flicks out the cigarette and then waves his hands to get rid of the smoke. He closes the double doors. He returns to the table to retrieve his whiskey glass. Then he goes over to the chest of drawers, carrying his glass. He places the glass on the chest and selects a vinyl record, 'Beautiful Lady Waltz' (1929), played in slow waltz time. He carefully extracts it from its sleeve and places it on the turntable. After a few crackles the music starts to play. HARRY keeps the volume down. He is coughing intermittently and is a little unsteady on his feet. There is a light knock on the door. NURSE Anna's unmistakable voice can be heard from outside.*

NURSE. Monsieur Clarke, may I come in?

HARRY. *(Flustered)* Oh…Oh just a minute Anna!

HARRY looks from the door to the whiskey glass, startled. He hurriedly shoves the glass behind the picture of his children on the chest of drawers. He has a quick look around the room. He heads towards the door, then stops suddenly as he spots the whiskey bottle and glass still on the table. He grabs up both, almost runs to the locker and shoves them inside. He gets a fit of coughing after his exertion but still manages to walk to the door. He pauses for a moment and struggles to take a few breaths before opening the door.

Anna, entrez!

NURSE *enters.*

NURSE. Ah, you are learning de French, Monsieur?

NURSE *is pushing a small trolley which contains various medicines, tablets and charts. She stops abruptly as she sees HARRY standing there, resplendent in a smart suit and tie, still managing to look handsome and dashing despite the ravages of his illness.*

Why, Monsieur Harry, you are looking so good this evening. (*Smiling radiantly*) You look like you are going to de Ball. I am so happy to see this! And you have your beautiful music playing once again. How I love those waltzes. I love to listen to them in my room at night.

HARRY. Good evening Anna, and many thanks for your kind words (*smiling ruefully*) but I fear the true expression should be more like 'death warmed up'. And you of course Anna, you are looking delectable as usual. You would certainly be the belle of any Ball. (S*miling coyly*) Now tell me Anna, do you like to dance?

Without waiting for an answer, HARRY goes over to the gramophone and puts the needle back to the start of the tune. The waltz begins again.

NURSE. Ah! Monsieur. (*Sighing wistfully*) Every woman would love to be the Belle of the Ball, at least one time...but sadly, I have spent most of my life working on my father's little farm and when I was not doing that I was nursing, so alas, I never had de time to think of such fancy things. I suppose you could call me Cinderella, Monsieur...without de handsome Prince though, I am afraid.

HARRY. Well then, Cinders (*Smiling impishly*) tonight you shall go to the Ball!

HARRY *raises the volume of the record, then he moves swiftly towards Anna, taking her hand, then bowing from the waist.*

May I have this dance, Mademoiselle? It would be such a pity to waste the fine music.

NURSE. Monsieur Harry! (*Squealing with delight*) Monsieur, what are you doing? I think you have gone quiet mad.

NURSE *giggles as* HARRY *takes her other hand. He leads her around the floor. They move awkwardly at first but then gradually they blend together as they both get used to the rhythm of the waltz.*

Oh! You move so gracefully, Monsieur. I am sure you must have danced with many fine ladies in past days.

HARRY. Well, I am certain I have never danced with one more beautiful than you Anna and you are so light on your feet, just like a little bird.

NURSE. *(Laughing with embarrassment)* If that were only true, Monsieur, you really are the flirt. I must tell you that I have only ever danced de waltz with my younger sister Eva. That is how I learned how to do it.

As they take another turn around the floor HARRY *holds* NURSE *closer, totally captivated by her charm and beauty. Suddenly* NURSE *appears to come to her senses and slowly pulls away from him.*

Please, Monsieur Harry, I thank you but that is enough now.

NURSE *stops abruptly. She pats her cap and hair to make sure she is not dishevelled. Her cheeks are rosy from the exertion of the dance and the excitement of the moment.*

I do not believe what I am doing here. (*Shaking her head, looking down and trying to compose herself*) Do not forget Monsieur, I am your nurse! Now please sit down. You should not be exerting yourself like this. And also Monsieur Harry, do not think that I have not noticed the smell of whiskey from you.

NURSE *looks sternly at* HARRY, *as she stands with*

both hands on her hips, but as she turns towards her trolley a little smile appears on her face. NURSE *speaks to* HARRY *over her shoulder as she fetches a new bottle of medicine.*

You know you really try my patience, Monsieur Harry.

HARRY. Forgive me, Nurse. *(Trying to suppress a fit of coughing)* I am sorry. I did not wish to upset you.

NURSE. You could never do that Monsieur Harry. *(Looking at* HARRY *with deep compassion)* That is, unless you refuse to take your medicine! *(Holding up the bottle of medicine)* I am leaving you a fresh bottle and some tablets to help you sleep.

NURSE *walks over to the locker, puts down the new medicine bottle and tablets and takes up the old ones. She places these on the trolley.*

I must take your temperature now and check your chart Monsieur.

NURSE *takes a thermometer out of her apron pocket. She proceeds to take* HARRY's *temperature. After a few seconds she removes the thermometer and takes a reading. She records this on the chart.*

(Frowning) This reading is high, Monsieur. I am serious now. You really must try to get more rest. Perhaps you should lie down now for a while.

HARRY. Thank you, Anna, but I am all right here for the moment.

NURSE. (*Smoothing down her apron*) Well, I must go now Monsieur Harry, as I expect the Professor will be around shortly and I must try to keep ahead of him, with my rounds.

HARRY. Ah, Von Botch is on the way. (*Smiling*) I wonder what fiendish ideas our dear demented Professor has in store for me this time.

NURSE. Monsieur, you should not call him that name…It is wrong…and I worry that the next time I see him I might call him that by a mistake!

NURSE *puts a hand over her mouth to suppress a laugh.* HARRY *laughs too.*

HARRY. Ha! I would like to see his face if you did, Anna.

NURSE. (*In mock irritation*) Monsieur, you want me to lose my work. (*Smiling*) You are such a funny man, Harry.

HARRY. Wow Anna! That is the first time you called me just plain old Harry.

NURSE. Oh, I do not know what I am doing or what I am saying when I am around you, Monsieur (s*ighing and shaking her head*).

HARRY. Oh! Before you go Anna, I…eh…I have

something for you (*leaning over to pick up the rolled-up sketch*).

NURSE. (*Frowning*) What is this, Monsieur?

HARRY. Why don't you open it and see?

HARRY *looks at NURSE as she carefully unties the bow and slowly unrolls the sketch.*

NURSE. (*Delighted*) Ah! Monsieur Harry, I can't believe this! It is amazing. You make me look so...so beautiful. Oh Harry! Thank you so much. Nobody has ever given me anything like this before.

NURSE *reaches over and kisses* HARRY *on the cheek. Then she draws back, blushing with embarrassment.*

Oh! I am so sorry, Monsieur! What must you think of me?

HARRY. I think you are marvellous, Anna. (*Reaching for her hand*) You are a pearl in this sea of sadness and decay. Don't you see Anna? (*Looking up at her with eyes full of sadness*) This place would be utterly unbearable if it wasn't for your presence.

NURSE. (*Struggling to regain control*) Please, Monsieur, I thank you for these nice things you say but I...I must go now. (*Stammering*) I have other patients waiting.

NURSE *moves hurriedly to the door, pushing the trolley*

in front of her. She turns at the door clutching the rolled up picture to her chest. She looks at HARRY for a moment with misty eyes.

I will treasure this forever, Monsieur Harry. It is such an honour for me…from such a great artist…and, and such a dear sweet man. Goodnight Monsieur Harry.

NURSE closes the door behind her. HARRY leans over the table and puts his hands over his face and shakes his head from side to side. As he hears NURSE Anna's light footsteps slowly fade away down the hall, he speaks in a barely audible voice.

HARRY. Goodbye Anna…Goodbye!

HARRY starts to cough badly. He puts a handkerchief to his mouth and finds it hard to breathe. He stands up now feeling an overwhelming mixture of loneliness, sadness, anger and self-pity. He continues to cough as he lurches over to the chest of drawers where he had hidden the whiskey glass. He bangs his knee on the side of a chair as he staggers across the room and he lets out a string of obscenities in frustration.

Damn you all. Damn you all to hell!

HARRY reaches over to retrieve the glass but he misjudges this and accidently knocks over the glass and his children's photo. Both shatter on the ground.

HARRY *jumps back in shock and horror.*

(Crying out) No!

HARRY *stares at the shattered picture for a moment before getting down on his knees. He carefully extracts the photo from the shattered glass, kisses it and brings it to his chest. He closes his eyes.*

(Anguished) I am so sorry, so sorry. Please forgive me. Please forgive me my darlings *(rocking back and forward on his knees, coughing and crying).*

The room darkens. An image of the devil from 'The Last Judgement' suddenly appears on the double-doors. A loud, booming voice accompanies the image.

MEPHISTOPHELES. Ha-ha! Come, Harry! Have you not led this life quite long enough?

HARRY. (*Tormented*) Let me be.

MEPHISTOPHELES. Come! Useless talking, delaying and praying! My horses are neighing: The morning twilight is near. Come hither to me!

HARRY. Satan, leave me be!

MEPHISTOPHELES. (*Commanding*) Come! Let us journey to the lake of fire. Ha-ha-ha-ha!

HARRY *covers his ears with his hands and drops to the floor, coughing and spluttering.*

Lights down.

ACT TWO

Scene ONE

Lights up on HARRY's *Room in the sanatorium. It is evening. An open case already half full is on the bed.* HARRY *takes a shirt from the wardrobe and carries it over, placing it in the case. He then walks back across the room. When he is walking past the gramophone he hesitates, looks at it, then takes the vinyl record off of the turntable. He places it in its sleeve. He takes out a brown paper bag and some twine from the drawer. He walks over to the table, takes up a pen, pauses for a moment and then writes a message on a sheet of notepaper. He places the note in an envelope, then puts the record and the note in the bag. He writes something on the bag and ties it with twine. He places this on top of the right hand locker beside the bed. There is a knock at the door.*

HARRY. (*Glancing up from his task of packing*) Who is it?

VOICE. (*Commanding, with a German accent*) It is Professor Gauche, Herr Clarke. May I enter please?

HARRY. (*Gathering up the half-packed case and sliding it under the bed*) Oh! Eh yes, of course Professor, come in.

PROFESSOR GAUCHE *enters, carrying a small attaché case, with a stethoscope around his neck. He walks smartly to the centre of the room. He gives a customary nod and clicks his heels. He places his case on the table.*

PROFESSOR GAUCHE. Ah Herr Clarke! How are you this evening?

HARRY. (*Smiling briefly, looking tired and wan*) I am as well as can be expected, Professor.

PROFESSOR GAUCHE. May I? Could you unbutton your shirt front please sir.

HARRY *does as requested.* PROFESSOR GAUCHE *places the stethoscope on* HARRY's *chest. He listens intently as he moves the instrument around, while asking* HARRY *to breathe in and out and to cough at certain times.*

PROFESSOR GAUCHE. Thank you, sir.

PROFESSOR GAUCHE *starts pacing the room as he slowly takes the stethoscope from his ears and places it around his neck. As* HARRY *buttons up his shirt, he stops pacing. He takes out a file from his case and opens it. After a few seconds spent scanning the file he closes it.*

Could you get your thermometer and weekly record please, Herr Clarke?

HARRY *walks to the right-hand locker to get the thermometer and the records. He brings them over to* PROFESSOR GAUCHE *who then places the thermometer in* HARRY's *mouth as he checks the record. He then checks* HARRY's *temperature.*

PROFESSOR GAUCHE. (*Frowning*) Mm...I see your temperature has been up these last few days, Herr Clarke. We must watch this. (*Glancing again at the file, then looking directly at* HARRY *with a serious expression*) Remember how we discussed the deterioration of your lung capacity after your last examination, Herr Clarke?

HARRY *nods and begins to rub his forehead, as though relieving a headache. The Professor continues.*

Well Sir, I feel at this time your right lung is only functioning at one-third of its capacity and it has not been responding to ze present treatment. (*Pausing for a moment before continuing*) While your left lung is not as bad, it is still showing similar signs of...deterioration. (*Placing the thermometer and the record on the table*) Herr Clarke we have been eh...experimenting with some new medication for a while now and it is working very well for some of our patients. I recommend that we start you on a course of this for, let us say, two months and then we will, eh, review the situation. *(Straightening up and placing his hands behind his back)* Are you agreeable to this sir?

HARRY. *(Looking directly at* PROFESSOR GAUCHE *with an air of calmness and certainty)* Professor...I have decided to leave.

PROFESSOR GAUCHE. *(Stunned, hardly comprehending what he is hearing)* What do you mean, Herr Clarke?

HARRY. *(Determined)* I am leaving here, Professor. I have made up my mind. I am checking out as soon as my friend arrives.

PROFESSOR GAUCHE. But, but you cannot be serious, Herr Clarke.

PROFESSOR GAUCHE's *monocle pops out suddenly and falls to his chest.*

Perhaps it is ze bad news I have just given you...Yes, that is it! Please do not be hasty, sir. *(Beseechingly)* There are so many things that we still have to try, Herr Clarke.

HARRY. *(Sincerely)* Professor, I thank you for all you have done, but I am tired of it all now. I just want to go home....to my children, to my wife and to my work. There is so much I need to do...I have important work to finish while I still have time. I need to leave, I hope you understand that Professor.

PROFESSOR GAUCHE. (*Sympathetically*) Herr Clarke, even if I do understand some of your motives, you are not capable in my opinion to undertake ze journey. (*Becoming animated*) Why, it is just folly to even think of such a thing…in this weather. You are even carrying a high temperature at this time…with the threat of pneumonia. Please, Herr Clarke, please reconsider. Why, will you not wait for the spring? Yes, the spring or the summer. Why, it would give us time to work with these new formulas.

HARRY. (*Shaking his head*) I am sorry, Professor Gauche, but I happen to have one of my friends already here at this time and I await the arrival of another. They will both be accompanying me.

PROFESSOR GAUCHE *paces the floor, his hands behind his back and a defeated expression on his face. He pauses at the double doors to look out at the weather and shakes his head.*

If your mind is made up Herr Clarke, there is nothing more I can say. (*Stopping and turning to face* HARRY) I will be working late all this week. If you would please call in when you are leaving so we can settle up everything. I will give you any files you need and extra supplies of medicines and some other things to aid you on your journey. (*Bowing, clicking his heels, heading for the door, then stopping and turning around*) Herr Clarke, should you decide to reconsider your actions, I would be very pleased. (*Looking concerned*) But I will leave you now. Good evening!

HARRY. Good evening, professor.

PROFESSOR GAUCHE *picks up his case, bows and exits.*

HARRY *sits on the bed for a few moments in deep thought. Then he pulls out the case from under the bed and opens it, to resume packing. Suddenly he begins coughing, until it is quiet uncontrollable. He walks in to the bathroom, leaving the door ajar and there is the sound of water running and splashing.*

There is a knock at the door.

LENNOX. Harry, old man. I'm back!

HARRY, *looking pale and tired, emerges from the bathroom holding a handkerchief and goes to open the door.*

(*Smiling weakly*) Welcome back, Lennox.

LENNOX *enters the room, carrying a small tray covered over with a cloth.*

HARRY. I was wondering for a moment if I'd imagined you were ever here. (*Putting a hand on* LENNOX's *shoulder and walking with him to the table).* The side effects of these medications old Botch has me on lately are causing me all kinds of problems...I find my mind wandering off at times.

LENNOX. (*Putting the tray on the table*) I'm as real as you'll get in this God forsaken place, old man! (*Uncovering the tray that contains a plate of sandwiches, a glass of milk and several serviettes*) Now, tuck in. You could do with a good feed.

LENNOX *pulls out a chair for* HARRY. *He places a serviette on* HARRY's *lap. He looks over at the bed and sees the open case, already half-packed.*

Bon appetite, old man!

HARRY. Thanks, Lennox. You're really too kind. I'm not that hungry but I'll nibble away. Did you get something yourself?

LENNOX. Lord yes, I was simply famished so I ate them out of house and home. Drank a nice few glasses of Beaujolais as well.

HARRY. (*Drinking the milk*) Can I get you something to drink Lennox?

LENNOX. *(Sitting down at the table across from HARRY)* You know I never come unprepared, old boy*! (Taking out a small silver flask from his inside jacket pocket and taking a drink).*

HARRY. (Chuckling) I'm well aware of that, my friend.

HARRY *takes up his glass and drinks his milk. For a few moments he becomes lost in thought.*

Oh, you know I'm so looking forward to getting home. *(Gesturing to the bed)* You can see I've already started packing. I've missed everyone so terribly.

LENNOX. You've been sorely missed by all your old buddies, Clarke, make no mistake.

HARRY. Oh! Do tell me what's been happening these past few months. But first, I must ask how your good lady is.

LENNOX. Oh! Dolly is very well indeed.

HARRY. *(Smiling)* So all is still rosy with you too then?

LENNOX. It certainly is, old man.

HARRY. *(Jovially)* Glad to hear it. And how is Hester? Still conversing with the spirit world?

LENNOX *(Smiling).* Ah! You know Hester, she still holds her séance every week. She's attracted some illustrious clients over the years, even Stoker.

HARRY. (*Coughing into a handkerchief*) Excuse me Lennox.

HARRY *has a fit of coughing.* LENNOX *stands up and goes over to him.* LENNOX *looks frustrated that there's nothing he can do to help. He walks over to the locker and fills the glass from the carafe of water. He carries it back to* HARRY. HARRY *tries to compose himself by taking in a few deep breaths. Then he takes a sip of water.*

Thanks, I'll be grand in a minute.

(*Clearing his throat*) Eh, I suppose Yeats still attends her circle?

LENNOX. (*Sitting back down*) He drops in from time to time. Of course to Yeats the spirit realm is more real than anything in this world. (*Taking another sip from his flask*) You know, Harry, I've never really understood you're thoughts on the afterlife. (*Pausing*) I've always put it down to the Jesuits. God, they must have scared you witless with their sermons on fire and brimstone.

HARRY *stands up, fidgeting with his handkerchief. Then he begins pacing up and down the room. After pausing for a few moments he begins to speak softly.*

71

HARRY. Yes, Lennox, you are right...Hell has always filled me with terror.

LENNOX. (*Folding his arms, speaking seriously*) I know, old boy. Of course the great irony is that hell and death seem to fascinate you so. I mean, you've spent much of your life immersed in visions of heaven and hell, creating memorials to the dead...not to mention your illustrations for Faust and Poe. (*Sarcastically*) Now, they were a tasty bit of work.

LENNOX *opens his silver case and offers a cigarette to* HARRY. HARRY *hesitates for a moment but then takes one, smells it longingly, then puts it down on the table.* LENNOX *takes out another.*

HARRY. Thanks, maybe later.

LENNOX *closes the case and then taps it with the cigarette. Then he places the case back in his pocket.*

Yes, later perhaps (*putting his cigarette on the table*). Well, you know where I stand on this by now, Harry. There is no death. Nor is there a hell full of wicked devils. Those exquisite angels you've spent decades perfecting, they're a symbol of what we all aspire to become.

HARRY *picks up the water glass from the table and takes a drink. He holds the glass in his hand and remains standing while speaking.*

I can never picture myself in the role of saint or angel, Lennox. At best, I place myself as a mere mortal, at worst the plaything of demons.

LENNOX. (*Softly*) But surely you must know, Harry, how your creations have given so much comfort and joy to many. If anyone deserves their just reward, it has to be you. (*Smiling*) Sorry, old man, no fire or brimstone for you!

HARRY. (*Pausing to sip the water*) Thanks, Lennox. Maybe 'tis the night that's in it and being so damnably far from home, but I'd rather fill my thoughts with angels than dwell on devils.

HARRY *walks over to the chest of drawers, fingering the body of the gramophone.*

Now if you don't mind Lennox, let's come back down to earth for a while. (*Leaning on the chest of drawers, looking upwards in happy thought*) Transport me to a sunny day in Grafton Street, drinking coffee in Bewley's surrounded by our old chums, catching up on all the news.

LENNOX: (*Smiling*) Well now, Harry, it just so happens I have a little snippet here to keep you going! (*Shifting in his chair to face* HARRY) It concerns our dear friend, Mr Yeats. He's planning a radio broadcast, you know. He's going to recite 'The Lake Isle of Innisfree' (*Slight chuckle*). I'd say people will get a bit of a shock when they hear his lilting tone—almost like an ancient chant.

LENNOX *recites the first line slowly in chant form, with mock solemnity.*

I will arise and go now and go to Innisfree.

HARRY *and* LENNOX *recite the second line slowly together.*

And a small cabin build there, of clay and wattles made.

HARRY. (*Laughing*) 'Tis a strange way he has of recitin', all right. I'd rather read his poems any day than listen to him droning on.

LENNOX. (*Looking directly at* HARRY *who is now yawning*) Am I tiring you out, old man? If you want to rest for a while I can go down and sort out my lodgings. I've secured a room down in the village.

HARRY. Ah, just stay another while, Lennox. It's so great having you here.

74

HARRY *walks back over to the table and sits down in the chair.*

Tell me, how is Lady Gregory?

LENNOX *takes up his flask, stands up and begins to walk around the room.*

Poorly I'm afraid. The grand old lady is bed-ridden now. She's asked me to edit her journals so of course I'll be honoured. Lady Gregory has always been good to me. I'll do anything I can to be of service.

HARRY. I always remember you saying how she stood by you over that unpleasant situation—when you kept the Abbey open during the King's visit.

LENNOX. (*Taking a sip from the flask*) Yes, there were many who wanted my head over that incident but the good Lady never flinched. She hardly knew me at the time yet she stood by me.

HARRY. I don't think we'll ever forget a pal who stands by us in our hour of need.

LENNOX. No, my friend, 'tis true. Where would we be without friends, eh?

HARRY. (*Looking directly at* LENNOX) We'd be lost Lennox, devoid of all hope.

LENNOX *walks over to the painting hanging on the wall and studies it.*

Ah, Margaret must have painted this when she was here last.

HARRY. Yes. She painted a few landscapes. The snow was quite a novelty for her. She really captured the light very well, don't you think?

LENNOX. (*Nodding*) She certainly did. What an exceptional artist she is?

HARRY *puts a hand to his forehead and squints as though in pain.*

Oh! I wish I was back home now. I can't wait to see everyone again.

HARRY *stands up and walks slowly over to the window.* LENNOX *follows behind him.*

LENNOX. You need to save all your energy...for later.

HARRY *and* LENNOX *look out at the falling snow in the ever-darkening landscape.*

LENNOX. (*Sipping his brandy from the flask*) It's so beautiful, Harry!

HARRY. Beautiful, yes.

HARRY *turns away from the window.*

But hell can have many disguises.

HARRY *walks to the front of the room.*

The mountains, skies and trees may seem all new and

strange to you but I'd rather have the view from my sitting room window than all the grandeur of the Alps.

(*Stopping to look at* LENNOX) I think I'm going mad here. I sometimes think I've already cracked, what, with all the concoctions they're pouring into me. (*Pacing again*) And then it's the same bloody thing every day.

HARRY *points towards the window.*

We sit around outside all wrapped up like mummies and we're forced to listen to Bankers, Blackguards and Buffoons talking about their losses on the stock exchange. (*Looking at* LENNOX) I can't wait to get back home, Lennox. I wish Duncan would come. Then we could all head off together. Just like old times, eh?

LENNOX. (*Turning around to face* HARRY) I wish to goodness you'd rest for a while, Harry.

HARRY. (*Coughing*) Ah! I'm sick of resting.

HARRY *gets a sudden fit of coughing and doubles over.* LENNOX *strides over and puts a comforting arm around his shoulders.* LENNOX *leads* HARRY *to the armchair and* HARRY *sits down.*

LENNOX. Take it easy, old man.

HARRY. (*Wheezing, breathless, gesturing towards the*

locker) Maybe some medicine, Lennox.

LENNOX *walks over to the locker and retrieves the medicine bottle and spoon. He brings them back over to* HARRY.

HARRY. *(Breathless)* Thanks Lennox.

LENNOX. (*Concerned*) Let me pour it for you, Harry.

HARRY. (*Waving him away)* It's all right, I can manage, thanks.

HARRY *proceeds to take the medicine. Simultaneously* LENNOX *walks over to the gramophone and browses through the small record collection, while still keeping an eye on* HARRY, *a concerned expression on his face.* LENNOX *selects a record. He places this on the turntable and turns the handle on the gramophone several times. The First Movement of Beethoven's Piano Sonata No. 14 (Moonlight Sonata) plays in the background.*

HARRY. (*Weakly, forcing a smile*) Ah, Moonlight sonata. Well chosen.

LENNOX. I thought it would suit your mood.

HARRY *nods.*

(*Dejected)* It's been a hell of a time these past few months (*downcast).*

LENNOX. (*Softly, looking directly at* HARRY*)* I take it there's been no word yet about *The Geneva*?

HARRY. (*Shaking his head*) There's been nothing whatsoever from Cosgrave. I really think they'll reject the window, Lennox.

LENNOX *walks back over to the table. He leans on the table, opposite* HARRY. *He shakes his head then listens to* HARRY *with rapt attention.*

HARRY. (*Exasperated but also resigned*) They've left me hanging. They're too cowardly to tell me they're reneging on our agreement. And we could sorely do with the payment. You know Cosgrave wanted me to change the O'Flaherty panel? Imagine the gall to ask me to do that, at the eleventh hour, when the entire commission was completed!

LENNOX. (*Shaking his head*) Margaret told me as much. I could hardly believe it. But it's not the window they're rejecting Harry, it's the writers whose works you've depicted—so many of them have been censored.

HARRY *breaks down in a fit of coughing.*

LENNOX. (*Angry*) Anyway, I hope you told Cosgrave to go to hell.

HARRY. He wrote to me, you know, a damnable letter, saying it would be (*mock elitist tone*) 'undesirable' to include the O'Flaherty panel, that it would give 'grave offence' to many people. What do you make of that, Lennox?

LENNOX. (*Raging*) What a load of cobblers? 'Undesirable' be damned! That window is one of the finest pieces of art ever created. Cosgrave and the whole damned Irish State should be honoured to be represented in Geneva, or anywhere else, by such a glorious work.

HARRY. (*Softly*) Thanks, Lennox.

LENNOX. By God man, it's truly a remarkable piece.

HARRY. (*Taking a sip of water*) Ah! You're only saying that because your play is included! (*Smirking*).

LENNOX. (*Speaking in a mock arrogant voice*) Sure, that's one of the main reasons it's so amazing!

They both smile.

HARRY. (*Coughing suddenly, trying to catch his breath*) I think I put every last ounce of strength I had into that window.

LENNOX. (*Sadly*) I know, old man. How many nights did I find you exhausted, sitting over that great desk, slaving away under a blazing light, after working all day from dawn to dusk in the studio?

HARRY. (*Tormented*) I sometimes think I ended up here because of the hours I spent on that blasted window.

HARRY *puts his head in his hands.* LENNOX *goes over to* HARRY *and puts a hand on* HARRY's *shoulder.*

LENNOX. *(Passionately)* Well, if it's any consolation, there'll come a day when *The Geneva Window* will be prized every bit as much as *The Book of Kells.* *(Striding over to the front of the room)* It will represent all that is finest in Irish art. Long after Cosgrave and the whole bloody lot of them—those censorious bastards—are dead and rotting in their graves, your wondrous window will be venerated for all that is sublime in design and colour.

HARRY. *(Looking at* LENNOX*)* Thanks, Lennox. 'Tis true the characters are the finest I've ever created. I think I poured in large chunks of my soul to give them life and they have all flourished while I'm depleted. *(Standing up with the water glass in his hand)* Lennox, I want you to promise me something.

LENNOX. Anything Harry, you know that.

HARRY *coughs again, takes a drink and pushes his long fringe out of his eyes. He rubs his eyes and then sighs. He speaks in a shaky voice.*

HARRY. Should the...

HARRY *stares into his glass, gathering himself together, taking a deep breath and beginning to speak in a more solemn tone.*

Should the inevitable happen before I reach home, Lennox...Would you look after the immediate...eh... arrangements, and contact Margaret...Will you do that for me, my friend?

LENNOX *looks at* HARRY *with sadness and compassion, then places an arm around his shoulder.*

LENNOX. (*Sincerely*) Harry...no matter what happens...I will always be there for you...and your family...you don't even have to ask.

HARRY. Margaret has always been so fond of you Lennox...I'm sure she will be so glad to have your support.

There is silence as HARRY *drinks some more water and* LENNOX *sips from his brandy flask.*

HARRY. You know, Lennox, Margaret has always been such a strong, practical, level-headed woman. (*Smiling and giving a slight chuckle to himself*) Much more balanced than I ever was. She could tend to her painting, look after the house, help out with the running of The Studios and do a great job rearing the children. That allowed me to be totally immersed in my work. (*Shaking his head while a sadness descends*) An amazing woman! (*Shaking his head again*) A truly amazing woman. (*Beginning to pace the floor*) God, I miss the children so much Lennox...those little rascals. (*Pause*) I don't know if you quite understand Lennox, not having children of your own...but 'tis actually a physical pain...a pain deep in my heart. If I could only see them...hold them once more.

HARRY *coughs into his handkerchief, then takes another sip of water.*

LENNOX *leads* HARRY *back to the table.* HARRY *sits down and* LENNOX *sits in the opposite chair.*

LENNOX. (*Compassionately*) Harry, you must be strong now, my friend...You must be strong for Margaret and the children...no matter what happens...Do you hear me, Harry?

HARRY *looks at* LENNOX *for a moment and then forces a smile for his friend.*

Damn it, you're right man!

HARRY *takes a deep breath and straightens himself to his full height.*

I'm sorry, Lennox. What must you think of me, snivelling like a baby...I'm Harry Clarke, for Christ's sake (*Shouting*) Harry Clarke!

LENNOX *nods and laughs. He picks up the cigarette from the table.*

This time, my friend I really do need to smoke!

HARRY *nods and retrieves his cigarette from the table.*

Ah, I might as well join you, Lennox.

The music on the gramophone comes to an end. HARRY *beckons towards the double doors.* LENNOX *walks over to the gramophone and replaces the arm in its holder.* HARRY *pulls open the doors.* LENNOX *follows, taking out his lighter and then lighting both cigarettes.* HARRY *takes a few puffs but starts coughing. In frustration, he throws it out over the balcony.*

HARRY. Oh! What I'd give to enjoy a good smoke again.

LENNOX. God, it's freezing. This damned climate would put you off smoking.

LENNOX *takes a few puffs then throws his cigarette over the balcony and closes the doors.*

Maybe it's time to lighten the music a little. Shall I put on something from Gilbert and Sullivan so you can give one of your unique performances (smirking)?

HARRY. (Smiling) You old rogue, if only I had the energy I'd sing you a few bars, all right. Just wait until I'm back home!

HARRY *goes back over to the table.* LENNOX *walks over to the gramophone. He selects a slow band piece from 1930. He turns the handle several times and the music plays.* HARRY *tries to eat one of the sandwiches but pushes the tray aside.*

LENNOX. (*Taking out his flask*) To brandy and music!

HARRY. Brandy and music, you old Vagabond! (*Playfully, holding up his water glass and clinking* LENNOX's *flask*) I'd better stick to water for now but I can't wait to have a bottle of stout with ye boys back in Toner's.

They both smile.

You know, Lennox, there's so much I still want to do.

HARRY *stands up and begins to pace up and down the room.*

My head's bursting with ideas.

LENNOX. (*Settling back into the chair*) So tell me some of them, Harry.

HARRY. (*With eyes alight*) Ah, Lennox, I have commissions for windows to get started on. You wouldn't believe some of the plans I have...down right shocking!

LENNOX. And they thought *The Geneva* was risqué?

HARRY. There are so many illustrations I want to do and, apart from that, I see some marvellous possibilities out there with all these new inventions....you just can't keep abreast of them. Do you know that some fellow has invented a small film box that will eventually be installed in people's homes? It'll be just as common as wireless, they say, in a few years. And I see those American boys have started to make animation films. Oh now! That's something I'd love to try, Lennox…Imagine bringing my illustrations to life! Incredible! And Margaret told me she was at the opening of the first-all colour, all-talking film at The Savoy lately. Have you seen it Lennox?

LENNOX *nods and smiles, delighted to see the excitement and sheer exuberance on* HARRY's *face as he talks.*

LENNOX. I was indeed. 'On with the show' it was called. It was good Harry but it'll never match the excitement of an Abbey's first night!

HARRY. Oh, do I detect a hint of concern there, Lennox? *(Teasingly)* A bit of competition, perhaps?

LENNOX. Bring it on, old boy! Bring it on, I say. *(Laughing, then holding up his flask)* Ah, here's to more great times, Harry. You, Margaret, Dolly and I— we'll be up in the box again–it'll be the same as ever. We'll have a celebration that'll last a week.

HARRY. *(Raising his glass)* Oh! That would be so marvellous, Lennox.

The record on the gramophone comes to an end.

LENNOX goes over to replace the arm back in its holder.

HARRY. I really think I have a chance if I can only get back home. Oh! I do hope Duncan comes soon. I told the Professor I was leaving with both of you. He understands now.

LENNOX. (*Looking shocked*) What? (*Then immediately trying to calm down*) You told him then...Well, let's leave all that 'til Duncan arrives. In the meantime, Harry, you need to rest. I'll go and sort out my room and then I'll come back for a nightcap.

HARRY. (*Sitting down*) Well, maybe just a short rest then. You'll be back later?

LENNOX. I will.

LENNOX puts on his coat and takes up his case.

I'll see you in a while Harry.

HARRY. You don't know how much I've enjoyed this evening with you, Lennox. It's been a real tonic.

LENNOX. It's been great for me also.

HARRY. Until later then.

LENNOX exits.

HARRY stays sitting for a few moments. Then he stands up and hesitates as he walks past the gramophone. He stops, goes over to it, takes the record off and puts it in its sleeve. He then selects another record and places it on the turn-table. He turns the gramophone handle several times and the turntable begins to rotate. He places the needle on the record. A Celtic instrumental piece begins to play. HARRY carries the empty glass over to the locker and refills it from the carafe. He closes the travelling case that's still on the bed and puts it on the floor. He takes a sip of water then collapses onto the bed. He closes his eyes and begins to breathe softly, as though soothed by the music.

The room darkens considerably, except for the double-doors that begin to exude colour and light. The full Geneva Window begins to materialise. The colours from the window slowly spread out and appear to flow in rays across the bed. HARRY is enveloped in colour. He opens his eyes. He stares at the window and begins to gradually sit up in bed, enraptured by its beauty. Then a close-up of JOXER from 'The Geneva Window' is displayed on the double-doors. JOXER materialises from the window, rubbing his hands together, a bottle of whiskey sticking out of his right-hand pocket. He walks unsteadily across the room towards HARRY's bed. JOXER takes out the *whiskey bottle from his pocket and takes off the lid. He offers it to* HARRY.

JOXER. Would you like a swig, sir?

HARRY. (*Slowly sitting up in bed, mesmerised*) Er...er...no...thanks.

JOXER *takes a drink from the bottle. The music on the gramophone begins to play the introduction to 'Spancil Hill'.*

(*Smiling*) If you permit me sir, I'll give you wan of my shut-eyed wans.

JOXER *puts the lid back on the bottle and puts it into his pocket. He walks to the centre of the room. He closes his eyes and begins to sing along with the record. When he finishes singing the first verse of 'Spancil Hill', HARRY claps slowly, utterly spellbound. JOXER bows and fades into the darkness.*

At the same moment the music changes to a haunting Irish melody. In the semi-darkness, the DANCER from 'The Geneva Window', clad only in a dazzling diaphanous sheet, dances provocatively across the room. The centre of the room is bathed in dark pink rays, reflecting the colour of her veil. HARRY gets out of bed and slowly walks towards her as though in a trance. The beautiful DANCER gyrates sensually around him, slowly raising, then lowering her veil, barely concealing her perfect body. HARRY flops into the armchair, utterly transfixed by the alluring dance. The DANCER dances around HARRY. He stares longingly as she gracefully weaves her sensual magic. She begins to dance backwards towards the bed. HARRY stands up and follows her in trance-like motion. He lies back on the bed, a look of deep satisfaction spreading across his face. The room suddenly darkens and the music fades.

Lights down.

Scene Two

Lights up on HARRY's bedroom in the sanatorium. The double-doors are pitch black as night has fallen. HARRY is lying on the bed. There is a loud knocking at the door. HARRY opens his eyes and looks around the room.

LENNOX. Clarke, old man, I've brought back one hell of a surprise for you.

HARRY gets a sudden fit of coughing and is barely able to speak. He pulls out a handkerchief and coughs into it. Then he looks into it and shakes his head. He wipes his mouth, then quickly shoves the handkerchief back into his pocket.

HARRY. (Spluttering) Len...nox! (Coughing) I'll be...

right...there.

HARRY *struggles towards the door. He opens it.*
LENNOX *saunters in, followed by a tall gentleman in a
long brown trench coat and hat, carrying a case.*

HARRY. Duncan! Good God, man!

DUNCAN *puts down his case.* HARRY *grasps*
DUNCAN's *elbow with one hand while shaking hands
with the other.*

HARRY. Lennox, can you believe it? Finally, he's here!

LENNOX *takes off his coat and carries it over to the coat
rack. Then he walks over to the chest of drawers and
leans against it.*

DUNCAN: It's grand to be here, Harry.

> DUNCAN *walks into the room and unbuttons his
> coat.*
>
> I thought I was seeing things when I ran into Lennox
> in the bar. (*Turning towards* LENNOX) Then we had
> quite a...discussion, isn't that right, old friend?

LENNOX. Indeed!

HARRY. Well (*trying to stifle a cough*), this certainly calls
for a celebration.

HARRY *goes over to the locker and takes out the bottle
of whiskey and three glasses. He brings them to the table,
then goes back for the carafe of water.* DUNCAN *takes*

off his coat and places it on the coat rack. HARRY *beckons for* DUNCAN *to sit in the armchair.* LENNOX *carries over a chair from the bed to the table.* HARRY *pours three whiskeys, adding water to his own smaller measure.*

HARRY. I thought you'd never get here, Duncan. I was counting the days, sometimes the hours. Now that you're here (*getting emotional)* it means I can start on my journey home. I know you've only arrived, Duncan, but do you mind if we leave in a short while? *Standing up and pacing across the room)* There's a train at 20.50. We'll get to Paris by the morning.

LENNOX *looks across the table at* HARRY, *then his eyes lock on* DUNCAN.

DUNCAN. (*Sounding resigned)* Lennox and I discussed the journey, Harry. It's freezing out there, but I promise you we'll take care of everything. Travelling in daylight would be a much better plan, if you'd consider that...

HARRY. (*Pleading)* If we could only set out now, Duncan...I'll wear three coats if I have to. The train will be warm anyway. I've almost finished packing. I really need to get going now. (*Looking at* LENNOX*)*

The three of us could set off soon. Let's have that drink, Lennox.

DUNCAN *stands up.* DUNCAN *and* HARRY *hold up their glasses.*

HARRY. To home!

LENNOX *pauses then holds up his glass. They toast in unison. Then* DUNCAN *looks at* LENNOX *who resumes his position beside the chest of drawers.*

DUNCAN. Are you on for it then, Lennox? Are we travelling by the evening train?

Both DUNCAN *and* HARRY *stare at* LENNOX.

LENNOX. (*Spoken quietly*) That decision, I fear, is well out of my hands. You've already made up your mind, Harry. (*Looking at his watch*) If you want to make that train we'd better get moving then.

HARRY. (*Beaming*) Thanks, dear friends. I'll just finish packing.

DUNCAN. (*Eyeing the sandwiches on the table*) Does anyone mind if I have a sandwich? I don't think I'll ever feel full or warm again.

HARRY. (*Excited*) Of course, Duncan! Please clear the plate if you can manage it. I'm too excited to eat anything.

LENNOX. I'd better go then and cancel my lodgings. I'll

be back in a jiffy.

HARRY *goes over to the case and puts it back on the bed. He takes up the record that he has previously wrapped.*

HARRY. Lennox, can you leave this at reception, please?

LENNOX. Sure, Harry. (*Reading the inscription*) For Anna.

HARRY. Thanks, Lennox. A parting gift for a special friend.

LENNOX. (*Smirking*) You're secret is safe with me, old man.

Lights down.

ACT THREE

Scene One

Lights up on the STATIONMASTER's Office at the railway station in Arosa. DUNCAN and LENNOX enter the office, holding HARRY up between them. HARRY's eyes are closed and he is looking very pale and weak. There is a light dusting of snow on their coats and hats. A howling wind can be heard outside and snowflakes are being blown into the room. They help HARRY to the middle chair. Suddenly there is the shrill sound of the STATIONMASTER's whistle, accompanied by the chugging of the steam engine as it gradually builds speed and struggles to gain traction on the icy tracks outside.

DUNCAN. (*Glancing over his shoulder*) Thank you very much, sir. This is very kind of you.

The STATIONMASTER comes into the room from the platform and closes the door.

STATIONMASTER. Oh! Think nothing of it, Monsieur. Your friend will need some heat and comfort while you are waiting for de taxi. There is also some coffee boiling on de stove. I hope you like it strong and there are some biscuits in the canister on de shelf. Please help yourselves.

LENNOX. Thank you, my good man.

STATIONMASTER. I will tell you immediately when de taxi arrives, Messieurs. (*Looking at* HARRY) If I may say so, you were wise to disembark at this station as the sanatorium of Arosa is not far from here. Your friend looks very poorly. But it should not take too long...although the roads are bad tonight. My friend Igor will get you there safely...He is a very competent driver.

LENNOX. (*Taking off his gloves and walking over to the stove, warming his hands*) We are in your debt again, monsieur.

STATIONMASTER. (*Giving a little bow*) Your luggage is quite safe in the parcel office also. Now Messieurs, I must return to my work.

DUNCAN. (*Accompanying the STATIONMASTER to the door*) Thank you again.

The wind can be heard whistling and snowflakes blow inwards as the door is opened. The STATIONMASTER *exits.*

DUNCAN *closes the door. He takes off his gloves.* DUNCAN *and* LENNOX *take off their hats and scarves and open their coats.* LENNOX *reaches over to remove* HARRY's *hat and scarf and to open his coat.* HARRY *appears to be sleeping but he is also feverish.* DUNCAN *and* LENNOX *go over to the stove and warm their hands. Then they pick up some mugs from the shelf and pour coffee from the old pot on the stove. They both sip the coffee in silence, enjoying the momentary respite. Just then* HARRY *starts to cough and they both turn suddenly to look at him.* DUNCAN *goes over to* HARRY *and reaches inside* HARRY's *pocket. He takes out a handkerchief. He holds it up to* HARRY's *mouth until he stops coughing. He then takes another handkerchief from* HARRY's *pocket and dabs his forehead, wiping away the perspiration.*

HARRY. (*Weakly, half opening his eyes and trying feebly to look around*) Why have we stopped?

DUNCAN. (*Concerned, dabbing* HARRY's *forehead soothingly*) Easy, old friend.

LENNOX *also comes to* HARRY's *side, a worried expression on his face.*

(*Trying to sound jovial*) Everything's all right, old boy. We just had to stop for eh...fuel and water.

HARRY. (*Barely audible, closing his eyes*) Is it...is it the waltz? The waltz...

LENNOX *looks at* HARRY *with a pained expression.*

Er...yes. That's it...the waltz, dear friend, the waltz.

LENNOX *looks at* DUNCAN *for a moment and then shakes his head with a frustrated expression on his face. He then turns and goes over to the stove where he puts his hand into his inside pocket and takes out a silver brandy flask.* LENNOX *pours some of the brandy into his coffee. He holds up the flask to* DUNCAN. DUNCAN *nods and walks over to join him.* DUNCAN *holds up his mug and* LENNOX *pours in some brandy.*

LENNOX. (*Turning to* DUNCAN) Damn it Duncan, whatever were we thinking?

LENNOX *takes a drink, trying to keep his voice down but sounding angry.*

Or more to the point, what were 'you' thinking?

LENNOX *looks from* HARRY *to* DUNCAN, *making sure* HARRY *is still asleep.*

I mean…I was put in a position here. I knew nothing of this plan that you'd hatched between you. I was dead against this, you must know that (*sounding resigned).* But how in God's name he ever got you to agree to this, Duncan, I will never know.

DUNCAN *takes a drink then looks calmly at* LENNOX.

Now Lennox, you know Harry just as well as I do. He is nothing if not persuasive and I would do anything to help our dear friend. I mean, obviously I knew about

98

his underlying condition and that in itself was cause enough for concern when travelling but...having said that, I would never have gone along with this had I known he was on the verge of pneumonia. I'm afraid he kept that from both of us....that's if he knew himself how sick he actually was.

DUNCAN *takes another drink from his mug as he looks over at* HARRY *who is very feverish now and muttering incoherently.*

He is a very sick man, Lennox. That much I can tell. (*Looking grave*) It's going to take all of his reserves, I fear, to get to the sanatorium.

LENNOX, *wide-eyed, looks from* DUNCAN *to* HARRY, *realisation slowly dawning. He rubs his brow and shakes his head.*

My God!

DUNCAN. (*Looking off into the distance now*) Sadly Lennox, I have seen many forms of sickness and disease in my time...in Gallipoli and beyond. You could say I became a bit of an expert...as countless times I was called upon to hold and comfort a dying soldier in his last moments. (*Turning to look at* HARRY *with a sad expression*) Yes, I have lost count of the friends and colleagues that I saw succumb, not only to gunfire and explosions in those dastardly battles, but just as many to disease. (*Looking into the distance*) I still see those faces looking up at me with their pitiful eyes, imploring me to help them. (*Staring down at the floor*) A lot of them were mere boys for God's sake. (*Looking at* LENNOX*)* I still see them most nights.

DUNCAN *turns away from* LENNOX *and drains his cup. There is silence for some moments, apart from* HARRY's *ragged breathing and incoherent mumblings. Then* DUNCAN *clears his throat and straightens up to his full height, hands clasped behind his back, looking every bit the military man.*

Lennox (*Authoritatively*), there is little point in us arguing about what we should or shouldn't have done. Our objective now is to get our sick friend to the nearest sanatorium as best we can. So I'd appreciate it if we could work together to this end.

LENNOX *nods.*

Now, I'm going out to find the stationmaster and to see if there is any news of our taxi. It's time we were getting on the road. *(Looking over at* HARRY *with deep concern)* He is in need of urgent treatment, I fear.

(*Turning to* LENNOX) Perhaps you could try him with a few sips of that brandy, Lennox.

LENNOX. All right, Duncan.

DUNCAN *puts on his hat, gloves and scarf and fastens his coat before opening the door. Snow is blown inwards as DUNCAN exits.*

LENNOX *shakes his head and, with a sigh, goes over to* HARRY *who has started coughing again.* LENNOX *takes a handkerchief and holds it to* HARRY's *mouth.*

HARRY. (*In a moment of clarity, between coughs but barely audible*) What's happening, Lennox?

LENNOX. Take it easy now, Harry. Try not to speak. Everything is fine.

LENNOX *begins to dab* HARRY's *forehead with another handkerchief as the coughing subsides.* HARRY *is shivering now and also perspiring.*

LENNOX. (*Trying to sound upbeat*) Hey, old man! I'm just going to give you a sip of brandy. (*Holding the flask up to* HARRY's *lips*) This should warm you up.

HARRY *just about takes a sip before rolling his head to one side.*

(*Struggling to get the words out*) I...I'm not feeling the best, Lennox...so weak...sooo tired.

LENNOX. (*Misty-eyed, sitting down beside* HARRY *and putting his arm around his shoulders*) I know my friend, I know.

HARRY *and* LENNOX *sit there in silence for several seconds. Then suddenly the door opens and in comes* DUNCAN, *with more snow on his hat and coat. The wind can be heard through the open door.* DUNCAN *closes the door behind him.* DUNCAN *takes off his hat and gloves and warms his hands in front of the stove.*

DUNCAN. Brr...it's bitter out there. Good news though. The Stationmaster says he's expecting the taxi in about ten minutes, so hopefully we'll soon be on our way.

DUNCAN *walks over to* LENNOX *and lowers his voice, peering into* HARRY's *face.*

So how is he?

LENNOX. (*Looking ashen faced and very downbeat*) Ah, he's very poorly, Duncan.

DUNCAN. Well, all we can do now is to try and get him the help he needs. *(Sadly)* It's in God's hands after that.

DUNCAN *pats* LENNOX's *shoulder. Then he goes over to the stove.*

(Pouring a mug of coffee) You want any more of this

coffee, Lennox?

LENNOX. Oh! All right then.

DUNCAN *pours out a second cup of coffee.* LENNOX *walks over and takes out the brandy flask. He pours some brandy into both cups.*

DUNCAN. (*Smiling thinly*) That improves the coffee somewhat.

DUNCAN *carries over the cups and sits down beside* HARRY.

They both drink their coffee in silence.

LENNOX. (*Apologetically*) Eh, about what I said earlier, Dunc, regarding your plan to bring Harry home...I'm sorry, old man. You didn't deserve it...you've always been there for him...I know that.

DUNCAN. Ah, that's all right, I understand...you of all people should know you can never say 'no' to Harry Clarke.

They both smile at this and nod knowingly. They resume drinking their coffee.

DUNCAN. You know my original plan was to bring Harry south for some sun and rest. It always helps Belinda's breathing when we spend time on the Cote d'Azur. (*Looking at* HARRY *who remains sleeping*) I really hoped it would help him. (*Staring at the floor again, sounding sad and upset*) TB is such a damned curse.

LENNOX *nods. Both* LENNOX *and* DUNCAN *stare at the ground.* DUNCAN *drinks down the last of his coffee and then places the cup on the table.*

DUNCAN. (*Turning towards* HARRY) God, Lennox, I wish there was something we could do.

DUNCAN *stands up and walks over to the stove, warming his hands.*

All the time I was on the train from Davos I kept seeing the three of us and the hell of a time we used to have with Doran back home.

LENNOX *comes over to the stove and stands beside* DUNCAN.

(*Smiling wistfully*) Remember those nights, Lennox? How Clarke would sit there holding court, drinking back his bottles of stout, keeping us all in stitches with his witty stories. There was always a sparkle about him, a charm that everyone was smitten by.

LENNOX. I know, old boy. (*Brightening up*) And what about those gay afternoons, jaunting all over Killiney and Dalkey in his brand new motor?

DUNCAN. (*Smiling*) Marvellous times, eh Lenno?

LENNOX (*Suddenly sighing*) The best!

They both look over at HARRY *who is still sleeping feverishly.*

DUNCAN. (*Shaking off his melancholy*) Right, I'm going out again to get our luggage ready and to make sure I can get the taxi as close as possible to the door. (*Putting on his hat, scarf and gloves*) You best get Harry ready then. I'm sure it won't be long now.

LENNOX. Yes, better get him sorted.

DUNCAN *exits.*

LENNOX *walks over to* HARRY *and stands looking at him for a moment.* HARRY *seems to be very peaceful now although his breathing is still ragged.* LENNOX *decides not to try to waken him just yet so he puts on* HARRY's *scarf and hat, fastens up his coat and tries as best he can to put on his gloves.* LENNOX *then puts on his own hat and scarf and fastens up his coat. He holds his gloves in his hand. He sits down alongside* HARRY *to wait.*

A few moments later the door opens and DUNCAN *comes in, with snow on his hat and coat. The wind is whistling behind him.*

DUNCAN. Lennox, we're all ready to go. I've got the taxi practically at the door so let's not waste a moment.

LENNOX. (*Jumping up*) Right, let's go then!

DUNCAN *walks over to* HARRY *and takes hold of one of his arms while* LENNOX *takes the other.*

LENNOX. All right, Harry. We're ready to go home now.

HARRY. (*Eyes fluttering as he starts to awaken*) Home...at last.

DUNCAN. Just try to move your feet, Harry, that's all. We'll do the rest.

HARRY *tries his best to take the few steps to the door.*

LENNOX. That's it, you're doing fine, Harry...you're doing just fine.

LENNOX *and* DUNCAN *help* HARRY *to slowly exit while the wind whistles through the open door and snowflakes are blown into the room.*

Lights down.

Scene Two

Lights up on HARRY's *bedroom in the sanatorium in Arosa.* HARRY *is asleep in bed.* LENNOX *and* DUNCAN *are standing beside the table at the centre of the room, holding two coffee mugs.*

LENNOX. God, that was an ordeal. Well, at least he's sleeping now.

DUNCAN. Thank God for that. The doctor said he's given him something to make him rest.

They both look over at HARRY.

LENNOX (*Turning back to* DUNCAN*)* And you heard what he said? *(Solemnly)* 'The next couple of hours will decide'.

DUNCAN. (*Taking a drink, sounding downcast*) It's as I suspected, Lennox. He has a bad fever and the TB is at an advanced stage.

LENNOX. (*Glancing over at* HARRY) I've had a dreadful feeling from the moment I heard of the plan. I know Clarke wasn't in his full senses to make such a decision. But he so desperately wanted to get back home...

DUNCAN *puts down his mug on the table, then goes over to one of the armchairs and flops down, sighing.*

There was no stopping him. He would have travelled alone, you know that. He was absolutely determined. (*Pausing, rubbing his temples, then looking over at* HARRY) He's relatively calm now. Try to get some sleep, Lennox. I know I'm exhausted but you set out long before I did. God knows what this night will bring.

LENNOX *puts down his mug on the table, then walks over to the vacant armchair and sits down.*

107

Ah, I think I'm nearly beyond sleep. (*Slowly rubbing his forehead*) But you try to get some rest if you can.

DUNCAN (*Trying to find a comfortable position in the chair*) Thanks. I don't think I can keep my eyes open for much longer. But wake me if you need anything, won't you, Lennox?

LENNOX. I will, Duncan, I will.

DUNCAN *settles down and drifts off to sleep.* LENNOX *sits there, looking over at* HARRY. *All is still in the room except for* HARRY's *laboured breathing.* HARRY *gets a fit of coughing.* LENNOX *jumps up and goes over to the bed.*

LENNOX. (*Softly*) Are you all right, Harry? Is there anything I can get you?

HARRY *beckons towards the glass on the locker and* LENNOX *helps him to take a sip of water. His coughing subsides.*

HARRY. (*Feverishly*) Music?

LENNOX. (*Coaxingly*) Music, Harry?

HARRY. (*Faintly but persistently*) Music...It stopped...

LENNOX. All right, Harry.

LENNOX *looks over at the luggage. Then he walks across the room. He opens a large leather case and*

108

carefully takes out the gramophone. He then rummages through another bag that contains the records. He selects a record, then carries the gramophone and the record over to the press. He sets up the gramophone, takes the record out of its sleeve and places it on the turntable. He turns the handle several times. A haunting Celtic air drifts across the room. HARRY lays his head back on the pillow, soothed by the music. He appears to fall asleep. LENNOX looks over at DUNCAN and sees that he is still sleeping. LENNOX goes back to his chair, feeling satisfied that HARRY is sleeping. LENNOX quickly drifts into sleep.

For a moment all is silent, except for the Celtic melody playing on the gramophone. Then HARRY begins to toss and turn. His eyes open and he turns towards the window. The image of 'The Eve of Saint Agnes' window appears. This image is then replaced by Section 4 (Panels 9 and 10) from 'The Eve of Saint Agnes'. Panel 9 is then enlarged and displayed alone, depicting the heroine, MADELINE, dressed in a white nightgown and negligee, and carrying a lighted-candle. Suddenly the image fades and the window becomes dark, all except for the glittering light of the moon. Silently, the beautiful figure *of* MADELINE *steps into the room, lighted by moonbeams that cascade from the window.*

HARRY *struggles to raise his head from the pillow. He stares entranced at the beautiful apparition.* MADELINE *walks slowly towards the bed. She places the candle on the locker beside* HARRY. LENNOX *and* DUNCAN *remain asleep.*

HARRY. (*Wheezing*) Madeline.

MADELINE *draws closer to the bed.*

HARRY. (*Smiling, sighing*) My lady fair.

MADELINE *bends down slowly towards* HARRY *and he is enveloped by her long golden hair and her shimmering translucent negligee. They appear to kiss. Then* MADELINE *draws back, gazing at* HARRY *for several seconds before taking up the candle and walking back towards the window. She turns to smile at* HARRY *just before the moonbeams fade and she is swallowed in darkness.*

HARRY *slumps back down on the pillow.* DUNCAN *awakens and looks over at* HARRY. *He leans over to see if* HARRY *is sleeping.*

DUNCAN. (*Softly*) All right, Harry?

Satisfied that HARRY *is still sleeping,* DUNCAN *drifts back into sleep. All that can be heard is the record playing on the gramophone. Then* HARRY *begins tossing and turning again. His head turns towards the window and he half-opens his eyes.*

The first section of panel eight in 'The Geneva Window' is now depicted. The image of a blazing red sunset is then depicted as THE WIDOW *silently steps forward from the darkness, her beautiful head bowed in sadness.* HARRY *tries to raise himself up.*

HARRY. (*Overcome with emotion*) Margaret? You have come...

THE WIDOW *glides over to* HARRY. *She draws close to the bed, then reaches out to embrace him.* HARRY *clings to her.*

HARRY. (*Looking sad*) Tell them...the children...

HARRY *tosses and turns.*

THE WIDOW *places her hand on* HARRY's *forehead to soothe him. Then she turns and walks back into the darkness.*

HARRY *struggles to catch his breath. He begins tossing and turning again. The figure of* MEPHISTOPHELES *suddenly appears accompanied by a booming voice.*

MEPHISTOPHELES. (*Loud and commanding*) Come Harry! Come! It is time.

A flash of thunder rips through the room.

111

HARRY. (*Feverishly*) No!

LENNOX *and* DUNCAN *awaken. They rush over to* HARRY. DUNCAN *half kneels beside* HARRY *at the right side of the bed.* LENNOX *stands near the foot of the bed.*

MEPHISTOPHELES. Your carriage awaits…Hahaha!

HARRY *reaches towards the window, arms outstretched, using all of his remaining strength.*

HARRY. Get away!

DUNCAN. (*Alarmed*) Are you all right, old friend? (*Putting his hands on* HARRY's *shoulder*) We're here, Harry. You're safe.

HARRY. (*Pushing* DUNCAN's *hands away*) I'm not going. No!

LENNOX. It's just a bad dream, Harry.

The upside-down image of HARRY *from 'The Last Judgement' flashes onto the window.*

MEPHISTOPHELES. COOOMME…

HARRY. (*Cowering, putting his hands over his face*) No! Leave me be!

DUNCAN. Harry, we won't leave your side. That's a promise.

The image on the window gradually disappears. Then it slowly begins to glow with soft golden light. The rays of light fall onto HARRY's *bed. The music on the gramophone changes to a beautiful angelic melody.* HARRY *slowly lowers his hands and gazes at the light. He becomes calm and peaceful, a smile upon his face.* LENNOX *and* DUNCAN *remain by* HARRY's *side. The image of 'Our Lady of Sorrows' (From The Honan Chapel, 1917) appears.*

HARRY. (*Transfixed, staring at the window*) Mother!

The window suddenly glows with a brilliant light. A woman with grey hair tied in a bun and dressed in a long blue robe materialises from the light. She glides over to HARRY *and stands at the right hand side of the bed.* LENNOX *moves beside* DUNCAN. DUNCAN *wipes* HARRY's *brow.* HARRY *reaches to embrace his* MOTHER.

MOTHER *comforts* HARRY *in her arms, singing her lullaby.*

MOTHER. Sheen, hush. Oh! My treasure, my child.
    Sleep without sorrow, sleep.

HARRY's *head falls onto his* MOTHER's *shoulder.*

Slowly MOTHER *stands up and* HARRY *appears to awaken.* MOTHER *takes his hand.* HARRY *steps out of the bed, now dressed in white. They both walk slowly hand in hand towards the light. Finally,* MOTHER *and*

HARRY *are absorbed into the light. All that is left is a*
soft glow in the room. The music stops playing.

LENNOX. (*Sadly, sinking to his knees*) I think he's
gone, Duncan.

HARRY's *body remains in the bed.* LENNOX *and*
DUNCAN *kneel at the bedside with their heads bowed.*
Everything in the room fades to darkness, except for the
light falling on the gramophone. All that can be heard is
the record's needle still turning on the gramophone.

Lights down.

EPILOGUE

Harry Clarke died in his sleep in Arosa, Switzerland, on January 6th 1931, having left Davos in an attempt to travel home to Dublin. He was 41 years old. His wife, Margaret (nee Crilly), and his friends, Lennox Robinson and Captain Alan Duncan, attended the funeral in Coire. Margaret erected a simple headstone over Harry's grave. A custom in Switzerland deemed that, after ten years, a notice would be placed in the national newspapers requiring the family of the deceased to declare that they would continue to maintain the grave. Since the Clarke family had no knowledge of this, Harry's remains were disinterred and were buried in a communal area. The headstone was destroyed and no trace of it remains.

After Harry's death, the Harry Clarke Studios continued to create stained-glass windows until its closure in 1973. The Studios lacked the artistic brilliance and unique imagination of its founder. In 1988 *The Geneva Window* finally found a home in the Art Deco district of Miami, Florida at the Wolfsonian. It is now hailed as one of the finest stained-glass works of the twentieth century.

Lennox Robinson took some consolation that his dear friend would continue to live on in his wonderful creations:

People who write books and plays and poems have their work put away on shelves where they may lie for years, unopened and unread. Harry Clarke in the east end or transept of many a church in Ireland and elsewhere comes to life with every dawn and will have his daily resurrection.

BRIEF BIOGRAPHIES OF ACTUAL PEOPLE REFERRED TO IN DRAMA

HARRY CLARKE (1889-1931): Irish stained-glass artist and book illustrator (1889-1931). Clarke was born in Dublin on 17 March 1889. His father, Joshua, had established a church decorating business, J. Clarke and Sons, at the back of his home at 33 North Frederick Street. His mother was Brigid McGonigal from Co. Sligo. She was prone to chest complaints and died in 1903 at the age of 43. Harry's sisters Kathleen (Lally) and Florence (Dolly), later worked in the administration of the business. His older brother Walter managed the church decorative side of the business.

Clarke's time at Belvedere College left a lasting impression on him due to the strict religious dogma taught by the Jesuits and their sermons of abominable tortures in hell for those who sinned, particularly those who were sexually prurient. This may account for Clarke's delicate portrayal of saints, angels and heroines on the one hand and his fascination with the sexually perverted and macabre on the other, that revealed itself in some aspects of his work.

Clarke's artistic gifts were recognised early by his father, Joshua, and he was subsequently tutored by artist and craftsman, William Nagle. Clarke also attended night classes at the Dublin Metropolitan School of Art, where he studied under Alfred E. Child, manager of the stained-glass studio, An Túr Gloine. Such was the brilliance of Clarke's stained-glass work that he won three consecutive gold medals from 1911 to 1913, at the Board of Education's National Competition at South Kensington, London and was also awarded a scholarship to visit some of the most famous cathedrals in France.

Harry married Margaret Crilly from Newry, a gifted artist and teacher, in 1914. They honeymooned on Inishere in the summer of 1915. Walter Clarke married Margaret's sister, Mary (Minnie), in June 1915. Harry and Margaret had three children, Ann, Michael, and David.

In 1915, Clarke won his first major commission to create nine windows designed in the Celtic Revival style for the Honan Chapel of St. Finbarr, at University College Cork. This enormous commission took three years to complete and included a spectacular three-light window, depicting St. Patrick, St. Brigid and St. Columcille. When the windows were unveiled Clarke received rave reviews for the delicacy and brilliance of his creations.

What makes Clarke's work so unique is his brilliance as a graphic artist, his experimentation with the full spectrum of colour on glass, his excellence in the technical aspects of stained-glass combined with his sublime imagination. Clarke's genius as a colourist was matched by his artistic mastery. He was an illustrator of books for the London publishers, Harrap and Co. His book illustrations include *The Fairy Tales of Hans Christian Andersen* (1916) and Poe's *Tales of Mystery and Imagination* (1919). *The Fairy Tales* of Charles Perrault was published by George G. Harrap in 1922; *Ireland's Memorial Records 1914-1918* was published by Maunsel and Roberts Ltd., Dublin, in 1923. Clarke produced two sets of book illustrations for whiskey distillers, Jameson's of Dublin, entitled *The History of the Great House– Origin of John Jameson Whiskey* (1924) and *The Elixir of Life* (1925). From the mid-1920s Clarke's illustrations became darker, more grotesque and obscene. His illustrations for Goethe's *Faust*, published by George G. Harrap and Co. (1925), and *Selected Poems of Algernon Charles Swinburne,* published by John Lane–The Bodley Head (1928), contain erotic and overtly sexual imagery.

When Joshua died in 1921, Harry and Walter took over the running of the firm, with Harry focusing on the stained-glass side of the business. In 1924 they moved to larger premises at 6 and 7 North Frederick Street.

Commissions flowed in from all over Ireland and the United Kingdom, from the U.S.A, Australia, Africa and New Zealand.

Clarke was diagnosed with tuberculosis in 1929 and was advised to recuperate at the St. Victoria sanatorium in Davos, Switzerland. It was a lonely time for Clarke to be away from his family and friends. He kept in constant contact through correspondence with his sisters, sending sketches of windows that he continued to supervise. Besides his deteriorating health and the cost of staying in Davos while work in the Studios was piling up back home in Dublin, Clarke was greatly worried that his commission for the Irish State, *The Geneva Window* (1930) was going to be rejected due to his inclusion of writers whose work was censored by the Irish Free State.

Harry died in Arosa, Switzerland, in the early hours of January 6 1931, after leaving Davos the previous evening accompanied by his friend Alan Duncan, in an attempt to travel back home. He was just 41 years old.

Harry Clarke's contribution to the development of stained-glass in Ireland was immense. To put his achievement in context, his work is consistently ranked among the world's masters, such as Tiffany, Burne-Jones and the medieval colourists.

LENNOX ROBINSON (1886-1958): Lennox Robinson was born in Cork. He was a noted Irish playwright, producer and director of drama for the Abbey Theatre in Dublin, an essayist, short story writer and editor. His years in the Abbey were spent working closely with Lady Gregory and W. B. Yeats. Lennox was a very close friend of Harry Clarke. They shared many adventures together. In 1926, while Clarke was recuperating from injuries sustained in a serious bicycle accident, they travelled to York, Burgos, Seville and Tangier. When Clarke had to return to Davos in October 1930 due to his deteriorating health, Lennox accompanied him. They enjoyed a short respite in Paris before travelling on to the St. Victoria sanatorium in Davos. Lennox stayed with Harry for a week before returning to Dublin. When Harry died on 6 January 1931, Lennox travelled to Coire with Harry's wife, Margaret, to attend the funeral. He also wrote a brilliant obituary in the Irish Times (January 17 1931) for his dear friend that detailed Clarke's stained-glass legacy.

In September 1931 Lennox Robinson married Dorothy Travers Smith, known as Dolly, daughter of spirit medium, Hester (nee Dowden). Hester's sister, Ellen Duncan was the mother of Lennox's close friend, Alan Duncan. Lennox's marriage thereby made himself and Alan Duncan cousins-in-law. Harry Clarke depicted a scene from Lennox's play, *The Dreamers* in the fifth panel of *The Geneva Window* (1930).

ALAN DUNCAN (1895-1943): Alan Duncan was the son of Ellen and James Duncan. Ellen was a founding member and later president of the Arts Club in Dublin. The club became a haven for artists and writers such as George Russell (AE), Lady Gregory and W. B. Yeats. His mother, Ellen, was the first curator of the Hugh Lane gallery. His father, James, was an actor with the Abbey Theatre. His aunt, Hester Travers Smith (née Dowden), was a celebrated spiritualist medium. Duncan served in Gallipoli as a Captain with the Royal Welch Fusiliers. He contracted dysentery in 1916 and was transferred to a military camp at Aldershot. He was placed in charge of conscientious objectors at their courts martial. After the war Duncan returned to Dublin. He worked as an arts journalist, an administrator at the Abbey Theatre, a secretary to W. B Yeats and as a tour guide for Lunn's Travel Agency. In April 1924 Duncan married Belinda Atkinson. Early in 1925 they moved to Paris, becoming part of the Irish expatriate circle which included Joyce and Beckett. Duncan was a close friend of Clarke and, at

Clarke's request, travelled to Davos, Switzerland in January 1931 to accompany him home, although sadly, Clarke died on route in Arosa.

JOSHUA CLARKE (1858-1921): Father of Harry Clarke. Joshua emigrated from Leeds to Dublin at the age of eighteen. He set up a church decorating business at 33 North Frederick Street in 1886. He married Brigid McGonigal. The couple had four children, Walter, Kathleen (Lally), Florence (Dolly), and Harry. Joshua changed the business name to J. Clarke and Sons in 1892, after the birth of his two sons. When Harry graduated from the Dublin Metropolitan School of Art he was awarded a scholarship to visit French medieval cathedrals. Joshua travelled with Harry to Paris where they both marvelled at the exquisite medieval windows in Notre Dame Cathedral. Joshua Clarke died on 13 September 1921, aged sixty-three.

BRIGID CLARKE (née McGonigal) (1860-1903): Mother of Harry Clarke. Brigid McGonigal was born in Cliffony, Co. Sligo. She suffered from poor health for most of her life. She married Joshua Clarke and they had four children. Her youngest son, Harry, was particularly close to Brigid. She died in 1903 at the age of 43, when Harry was just fourteen years old. Both Harry and his brother, Walter, inherited the tendency towards ill health, particularly chest complaints.

MARGARET CLARKE (née Crilly) (1884-1961): Wife of Harry Clarke. Margaret Crilly was originally from Newry and won a scholarship to attend the Dublin Metropolitan School of Art where she trained to become an art teacher. Her artistic abilities achieved recognition with school awards and British Board of Education National Art Competition medals. She met Harry Clarke while studying at the Dublin art school. In the summer of 1913, Crilly, her younger sister Mary (Minnie) and Clarke's brother, Walter, joined Clarke and other artists on the island of Inishere. Margaret and Harry married on 31 October 1914 at the Pro Cathedral, Dublin. Walter subsequently married Minnie Crilly. Margaret was almost five years older than Harry. They had three children, Ann, Michael, and David. Margaret continued painting, achieving full RHA (Royal Hibernian Academy) status in April 1927 and establishing a reputation for her portraiture. Margaret completed a portrait of Lennox

Robinson in 1926. Margaret and Lennox remained close friends throughout their lives.

FLORENCE (DOLLY) CLARKE, born 1883: Sister of Harry Clarke. Dolly worked in the Joshua Clarke Studios. Dolly and Lally looked after the administration side of the business. From July 1930 Dolly continued to work in the Harry Clarke Studios. Dolly frequently corresponded with Harry about studio business when he was in Davos.

KATHLEEN (LALLY) CLARKE, born 1875: Eldest sister of Harry Clarke. Lally worked with Dolly in the offices of the Joshua Clarke Studios and, after Harry's death, in the Harry Clarke Studios.

WALTER CLARKE (1877-1930): Brother of Harry Clarke. After Joshua's death, Harry took over the running of the stained-glass section of the business while Walter looked after the church decorative side. Walter took over all business correspondence when Harry was away in London, travelling around Ireland working on commissions or when he first went to Davos in 1929. Walter became ill at Christmas 1929. In July 1930 Harry returned home to set up The Harry Clarke Studios. In that same month Walter died from pneumonia after a short illness.

HESTER TRAVERS SMITH (née Dowden) (1868-1949), was an Irish spiritualist medium who claimed to have contacted the spirits of Oscar Wilde, William Shakespeare, Hugh Lane and others. Hester wrote *Voices from the Void* (1919) and *Psychic Messages from Oscar Wilde* (1923). Hester's parents, Mary Clerke and Edward Dowden, both had family roots in County Cork. Her father was Professor of Oratory and English Literature at Trinity College, Dublin. Her sister, Ellen, married James Duncan and their son was Alan Duncan. Hester married Dr. Richard Travers Smith and they had one daughter, Dorothy Travers Smith, known as Dolly. Lennox Robinson married Dolly in September 1931. Hester held séances in Dublin that were attended by many artists and writers, including Bram Stoker and W. B. Yeats.

DOLLY ROBINSON (nee Travers Smith) (1901-1977): Wife of Lennox Robinson. Dolly Robinson was born Dorothy Travers Smith in Dublin, the daughter of Richard Travers Smith MD and Hester (née Dowden), the celebrated spiritualist medium. Dolly studied art in

126

London before designing sets for the Abbey Theatre. She set up a studio on North Frederick Street, Dublin, close to where Harry Clarke's studios were located. In September 1931 Dolly married Lennox Robinson. A charcoal portrait of Dolly by Margaret Clarke hangs in the Crawford Gallery in Cork.

BELINDA DUNCAN (née Atkinson): Wife of Alan Duncan. The Duncans had visited Harry in Davos in April 1929. Belinda was also consumptive and spent time in the South of France recuperating. Harry had initially planned to leave Davos with Duncan and to convalesce with the couple in the South of France. When Harry's illness became severe this plan changed. Duncan travelled to Davos and from there the pair planned to return to Dublin.

LADY GREGORY (*née* Persse) (1852-1932): Isabella Augusta Lady Gregory was an Irish playwright, folklorist and manager of the Abbey Theatre in Dublin. Although she was born into the privileged British class, she became strongly identified with cultural nationalism. Lady Gregory co-founded the Irish Literary Theatre and the Abbey Theatre with W.B Yeats and Edward Martyn. She wrote several short works and a number of books on Irish mythology. Her home at Coole Park in Co. Galway was frequented by many Irish literary Revival writers, most notably W. B. Yeats. Lady Gregory was manager of the Abbey Theatre when Lennox Robinson first became employed there. They formed a firm friendship. Lennox was asked by Lady Gregory to edit her papers after her death. These were published in 1946 as *Lady Gregory's Journals 1916-1930*. Harry Clarke depicted a scene from Lady Gregory's *The Story Brought by Brigit* in the first panel of *The Geneva Window* (1930).

WILLIAM BUTLER YEATS

William Butler Yeats (1865-1939) was an Irish poet and advocate of the Irish Literary Revival. He was fascinated by the occult. He was a co-founder of the Abbey Theatre. In his later years he served two terms as senator of the Irish Free State. In 1923, he was awarded the Nobel Prize in Literature. Yeats was asked by Harry Clarke to help him select fifteen of Ireland's finest writers to depict their works in *The Geneva Window* (1930). Clarke depicted Yeats' play, *The Countess Cathleen*, in the second section of the Fifth panel of *The Geneva Window* (1930).

FURTHER READING

The playwrights found *The Magic Mountain* by Thomas Mann [1924] to be of particular interest when researching the sanatoriums in Davos, Switzerland in the 1920s.

These books on Harry Clarke were essential reading to understanding the man, his work and his great legacy in book illustration and stained glass:

Dark Beauty: Hidden Detail in Harry Clarke's Stained Glass, Lucy Costigan and Michael Cullen, (Dublin: Merrion Press, imprint of the Irish Academic Press, 2019).

Harry Clarke and Artistic Visions of the New Irish State, Angela Griffith, Marguerite Helmers and Roísín Kennedy, (eds), (Dublin: The Irish Academic Press, 2018).

Harry Clarke: The Life and Work, Nicola Gordon Bowe (Dublin: The History Press, 2012; Irish Academic Press [1989]).

Harry Clarke's War: Illustrations for Ireland's Memorial Records, 1914-1918, Marguerite Helmers, (Dublin: The Irish Academic Press, 2015).

Strangest Genius: The Stained Glass of Harry Clarke, Lucy Costigan and Michael Cullen (Dublin: The History Press, 2010).

SONGS AND MUSIC REFERRED TO IN DRAMA

Bye Bye Blackbird (1926) by Ray Henderson and Mort Dixon, first recorded by Sam Lanin's Dance Orchestra in March 1926.

Beautiful Lady Waltz (1929), The Troubadours, conducted by Nat Shilkret.

Piano Sonata No. 14 in C♯ minor 'Quasi una fantasia', OP. 27, No. 2 (1801), (Moonlight Sonata), by Ludwig Van Beethoven.

Spancil Hill, by Michael Considine (1850-73).

ABOUT THE PLAYWRIGHTS

Anthony Costigan co-wrote and directed the documentary, *A Revel in Blue: The Life and Work of Harry Clarke* (2012). He is currently musical director for the documentary film *Journey Through Glass*, (Irishimages.org/film) to be released in 2020.

Lucy Costigan is the author of *Strangest Genius: The stained glass of Harry Clarke* (with Michael Cullen, The History Press, 2010), shortlisted for Best Irish Published Book by the Irish Book Awards in 2010 and nominated for Book of the Decade by Dublin Book Festival in 2016. Lucy is also the author of Dark Beauty: Hidden Detail in Harry Clarke's Stained Glass (with Michael Cullen, Merrion, 2019). Lucy produced *A Revel in Blue: The Life and Work of Harry Clarke* (2012) and is Director and Co-writer of the documentary *Journey Through Glass*, (Irishimages.org/film), to be released in 2020. Lucy's biography *Glenveagh Mystery: The Life, Work and Disappearance of Arthur Kingsley Porter* (Merrion, 2012) became a national bestseller.

Theresa Cullen was researcher on *Strangest Genius: The stained glass of Harry Clarke (2010), Dark Beauty (2019)* and *Glenveagh Mystery (2012)*. Theresa was Executive Producer for *A Revel in Blue: The Life and Work of Harry Clarke* (2012). Theresa is also Executive Producer for the forthcoming documentary film *Journey Through Glass*, (Irishimages.org/film).

CPSIA information can be obtained
at www.ICGtesting.com
Printed in the USA
BVHW081128050423
661803BV00005B/143